MW01062435

The Escape

Huguenot Inheritance Series #1

The Escape

The Adventures of Three Huguenot Children Fleeing Pesecution

(Based on historical facts)

by

A. VAN DER JAGT

INHERITANCE PUBLICATIONS
NEERLANDIA, ALBERTA, CANADA
PELLA, IOWA, U.S.A.

Canadian Cataloguing in Publication Data
Van der Jagt, A. (Anton), 1921-
   The escape
   ISBN 0-921100-04-3
   1. Huguenots - Juvenile fiction. I. Title.
PS3572.A45E8 1988   813'.54   C88-091441-6

Library of Congress Cataloging-in-Publication Data
Van der Jagt, A.
   The escape : the adventures of three Huguenot children fleeing
persecution (based on historical facts) / A. Van der Jagt.
        p.   cm.
   Summary: In seventeenth-century France, a young Huguenot
boy, his little sister, and a friend decide to escape to Holland
where they can be free of religious persecution.
   ISBN 0-921100-04-3 (pbk.) : $9.95
   [1. Huguenots—France—Juvenile fiction. 2. Huguenots—France
—Fiction.] I. Title.
PZ7.V28385Es   1993
[Fic]—dc20   93-38792
                                                                          CIP
                                                                          AC

Cover design and illustrations by Jaap Kramer

Published simultaneously in the United Kingdom by
Inheritance Publications (U.K.)

Published simultaneously in U.S.A. by Inheritance Publications
Box 366, Pella, Iowa 50219

Available in Australia from Inheritance Publications
Box 1122, Kelmscott, W.A. 6111 Tel. & Fax (089) 390 4940

Fourth Printing 2001

ISBN 0-921100-04-3

Printed in Canada

To my wife,

with gratitude and love.

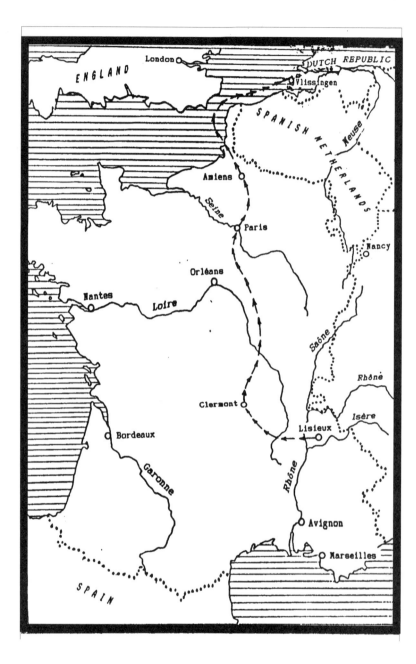

Table of Contents

1

THE INTERROGATION

"John, John, noon meal is ready!"

The girl who called had just come through the door of a small cabin, which stood in an open clearing of a large forest in the south of France. She was eight or nine years old, barefoot and wearing a simple gray frock. Not hearing John's usual whistle in reply to her calling, she yelled again, this time much louder. Still no response! He must be too far off, she thought, helping Daddy cut wood or watching the beehives. Without waiting longer she skipped away past the kitchen-garden and goat-shack along a narrow trail, which ended at another large clearing. She stopped a moment, screened her eyes against the bright sunshine, and looked across the clearing to the other side. When she saw both John and her father watching one of the beehives, she raced through the beautiful flowering heather, shouting, "Dad! Dad! John! You must come home! The meal is ready!"

Both looked up, and the father opened his arms just in time for she jumped right into them. He hugged her and then, smiling, let her slide to the ground.

"Well, well, my girl. What a high jump you made. You nearly threw your old daddy on the ground."

"Nothing doing," she said, laughing aloud. "You are so strong that nobody can topple you over. I didn't know you were here, Daddy. Is something wrong with the bees. Why are you looking at them?"

"John warned me that the bees of this hive may start swarming and we are trying to figure out if he is right. See how busy they are? There are many more bees at the entrance of this beehive than at the other ones! I don't think that they will swarm today, though. Maybe the bees crowd out because it is too hot inside. See, they are trying to bring cool air into the beehive."

She looked with a sudden interest at the opening of the beehive and saw a large number of bees all standing next to each other with their back ends up, flapping their wings.

"Oh, how funny it looks. Did you tell them to do it, John?" she giggled.

"Of course not, their king[1] commands them, doesn't he, Daddy?"

The father, ready to go home, picked a heavy axe up off the ground, swung it across his shoulder, and turned to leave along the trail.

"Yes, that's right. I told you so last week! But come on, children, don't make Mommy wait!"

"Let's run, John. I'll be the first one home!" the girl yelled cheerfully, and all at once took off as fast as her feet would carry her. John could easily beat her with his longer legs but purposely stayed a few steps behind, intending to let her win. The girl, however, couldn't keep up her pace, and slowed down before they were home. Stepping beside her, John grasped her hand affectionately.

"You know what, Manette? Daddy feels that we should get the honey out of that hive we were looking at and he promised to let me do it tomorrow! And if I do it well I can do the other hives, also, in a few months. Wouldn't that be fun?"

"Oh, John, Mommy baked bread today for we had nothing else to eat. Tomorrow, bread with honey. Delicious!" Manette licked her lips in anticipation of such a tasty meal.

"We have been so long without honey that I hardly remember its taste anymore," she added.

Their mother, a short woman with black hair and a friendly face, just came from the goat-shack and carried a pitcher with milk to the house.

"Is your father coming also?" she asked. Before the children could answer, he entered, put his axe against the wall, and hugged his wife as if he hadn't seen her for days.

"How good it smells," he said, amazed. "Did you bake bread today?"

His wife explained that it was impossible to wait longer with the baking because no other food was left. He nodded thoughtfully and seated himself on one side of the plain wooden table. His wife put bread on the table with the pitcher of milk and sat down also. The children, as was their custom, remained standing on opposite sides of the table.

---

[1] It was commonly thought that bees lived in a well-organized state, ruled by a king (the largest bee in the beehive). Jan Swammerdam (1637-1680), the famous Dutch entomologist, was the first one to discover that the largest bee is not a male king but a female queen, who lays all the eggs in the hive.

After the father had thanked the Lord for the food and asked for a blessing,[2] they began their sober meal. While they were eating, John told his mother excitedly about the beehive that his daddy was allowing him to smoke out because he felt that it had enough honey. Manette, who was still wondering about the bees having a king, wanted to know more about this and very soon a lively discussion developed. John was just explaining that every hive had one king only and that he was much larger than the other bees, when he stopped in the middle of a sentence, hearing an unusual sound outside.

The others also heard it and listened attentively. It was a rare occasion when somebody came to their cottage, so it was not surprising that they were amazed to hear distinctly the sound of a horse stopping in front of the house. John and Manette turned to the door, intending to run outside, but were stopped in their tracks by the voice of their father, who told them firmly to stay at their places.

"I'll see what kind of visitor we have," he told his wife. "Maybe it's a traveler who's lost his way."

He went outside and the children heard a brief exchange of words, which they couldn't understand, followed by the sound of a horse cantering away from the house. When their father entered again he looked puzzled.

"I don't understand what is going on," he remarked to his wife. "It was Alphonse. He didn't even dismount, and just said that Francis wants us all to come immediately. He was apparently in a hurry, for he turned the horse around while talking and galloped away. When I called after him to ask what is going on, he turned his head and yelled that we must hurry."

"Maybe Francis isn't feeling well or he got a letter from the Count as happened two years ago," his wife suggested hesitantly.

"Yes, that's possible but I fail to see why you and the children must come also. Well, we'd better hurry. Make yourself ready and let's go."

It didn't take very long before they were on their way to the village where Francis, the brother of John and Manette's father, was a priest. They walked a little more than two hours along a little-used trail before they arrived in the village of Lisieux. During their walk, the father and mother had been unusually quiet, sometimes shaking their heads as if trying to hide some worried thoughts.

---

[2] Private prayer, especially praying out loud at home, was considered to be a crime in France until 1750. Its punishment was death or a life term on the galleys. In 1685 in the city of Beaucaire, a minister, who had done nothing but pray to God, was hung.

Usually, the only street of the village was deserted at this time of the afternoon, but today a lot of people were standing in small groups talking together in subdued voices. It seemed that even some strangers were mixed in with the villagers.

"I never knew that the people cared so much for Francis," the father said in a low voice to his wife, thinking that his brother was ill and the people were discussing it. He approached one of the groups and asked them what was the matter, but some of them turned abruptly away and the others had peculiar expressions on their faces as if they were embarrassed to say anything. Father, impatient as he always was, didn't take the time to push for an answer but turned around and continued walking to the priest's house.

"No use waiting for these people," he muttered. "At Francis' we'll find out everything we need to know, anyhow."

The door of the house was wide open. Father hustled all of them into the hall, but before he was halfway to the study, two soldiers appeared from a small side-room, closed the door and remained standing in front of it. When Father saw the soldiers, he became pale and turned to his wife.

"The time has come for us to confess our faith in the Lord. Don't become discouraged! Trust Him for He will make everything well, Dear."

It was quite crowded in the study. John saw Poirot with his wife and children and also the smith, Armand, with his wife. After some shuffling around, everybody had a place. The adults all lined up against the wall and the children stood in front, all facing Father Francis and a foreign priest, who were sitting behind a large table. The foreign priest, who wore a beautiful, colored robe, was the bishop. He stood up, waited until everybody was quiet, and then began speaking with a very stern look.

He explained that a year ago, in 1685, their gracious king, Louis XIV, the Sun King, had repealed all the laws that protected the Huguenots[3] because he wanted them to return to the Roman Church.[4] He explained

---

[3] In 1598, King Henry IV of Navarre had given the French Protestants (Huguenots) a special law, the Edict of Nantes, in which freedom of religion and many other privileges were guaranteed. However, they lost most of these rights before 1628 and a short time later the persecution started again. King Louis XIV wanted to unite France and expected to achieve it by forcing the Huguenots into the Roman Church using any possible means, including bribery, exile, persecution, and murder.

[4] King Louis XIV of France (1638-1715) considered himself an absolute king. He felt that nobody ranked higher than he. He never said "I am the State" (L'etat, c'est moi), but he fully agreed with it. Therefore, he encouraged the people to call him the Sun King (le roi soleil) or the grand monarch (le grande monarch).

that Father Francis had called for his help to make sure that the Huguenots in Lisieux understood these things. For a long time the bishop continued his speech by elaborating vividly the punishment that heretics would undergo if they didn't repent. At last, with an unctuous smile, he finished his sermon by stating that the Roman Church understood their reluctance and was willing to make their return as easy as possible. As soon as they said to him and Father Francis, "I reunite with the Roman Church," everything would be alright. Later, legal agreements with the same wording would be drawn up which they, of course, had to sign and that would end the matter.

The adults objected strongly to his coercion and a long discussion followed, intermixed with a number of threats by the priests. At last, Poirot gave in, and his wife also consented to become a Romanist again. Armand, his wife, and John's father and mother didn't budge. They explained that they couldn't do it because the Roman Church wasn't the Church of Christ, and that the Lord Himself had recorded in His Bible that they were only allowed to join His Church and that He must be obeyed! Late in the afternoon, the angry priests realized that the Poirot family was the only one that was going to give in. They stopped their efforts and permitted the villagers to go home and reconsider their "heretical" attitudes.

Once outside the house, the Armands accompanied John's family for a while on their way home. John heard Armand ask his father why didn't he leave the country and he heard his father say that leaving was impossible because the children would be taken away from them and put into a cloister.

After the Armands had left them, John walked for a long time next to his father. They didn't talk but just before they were home, his father said softly so that his wife and Manette wouldn't hear it that he expected to be put in jail soon. He trusted that when it happened, John would act like a man and help his mother and Manette as much as he could. He added that John could be sure that the Lord would never forsake them in spite of the difficult times ahead of them all.

The next morning when John and Manette were deep in the forest, gathering wood for the fireplace some soldiers came to the cottage, handcuffed their father and took him away. He was sentenced to row on a war galley[5] for the rest of his life.

---

[5] War galleys were large, low ships rowed by convicts chained to the benches. Six men were allotted to each fifteen-foot oar, and were forced to hold a pace set by an overseer with a whistle.

2

A DIFFICULT CHOICE

The little village of Lisieux had always been a quiet place since it was very isolated in the southeast of France. Because of its location, most of the villagers knew little or nothing about the important events in the outside world, and often were not very interested in them, anyway. Travelers were the common bearers of all tidings, but rarely bothered to stop and talk. Often they just hurried through to the next village, seeing how small this one was. Everyday life in the village had always been dull and uneventful, even boring. Only once, four years ago had an extremely exciting event taken place when Father Francis had sent one of his own brothers and the smith of the village to the city jail where they were condemned to the galleys. For months the villagers had talked about little else but the fanatical action of the priest and the poor victims.

Today, a nice warm day in June, had not been different from any other day. From sunup to sundown the villagers had worked in the fields and were now eating their suppers. The only street in the village was deserted, except for a lonely boy, John, who walked along unhurriedly. His mother had died and an uncle and aunt had taken him into their house. They were warmhearted, easygoing people who treated him as if he was their own son.

Usually John came home at the same time as all the other villagers, but today he had purposely put it off as long as possible for he was afraid that his uncle and aunt would not welcome him in their typical good-natured way. He knew that they must have heard that, in spite of their frequent and urgent warnings, he had not attended Mass in the morning, and expected them to be angry with him.

He walked slowly past the first house in the street, a tiny, dilapidated building that resembled a shack. In fact, all the houses of the village were small and nearly all of them looked old and rundown.

The largest building was the brick church, which dominated the village. At first glance it seemed incredible that this small and poor community could afford such a beautiful church. The simple explanation was that Father Francis was not only fanatical, but also shrewd. He knew very well how to get the most out of his parishioners. Anyone who earned some extra money could be certain of Father Francis' appearance the next day to ask for his share, which he never used for himself but mainly for the beautification of "his" church.

The only other brick building in the village was the house of John's Uncle Louis, which had a neat and friendly appearance even though it was not large or new. John's grandfather had built it in his spare time, and it had taken many long years to complete. Most of the villagers were proud that they had such a nice, brick house in their village, and they highly respected John's uncle for it.

At this time of the day, Uncle Louis and Aunt Mary were having supper. They were sitting at the kitchen table, looking rather dispirited. Uncle Louis, deep in thought, was eating a piece of meat while Aunt Mary, without her usual smile, was cutting a slice of bread.

"Please, Louis, don't be too hard on the boy. You can hardly blame him for his disobedience after having been brought up as a Huguenot. I'm sure that he'll shape up if you give him some more time to think it over," she pleaded. Uncle Louis looked up, and seeing her worried face, tried to comfort her.

"Don't worry so much, Mary. You know that I am not going to beat him up because that won't help. It struck me the other day that John resembles his father when he was young, and I wouldn't be surprised if he is just as stubborn. Really, I haven't the faintest idea what to do. I think I'll have a quiet talk with him again but I doubt that it will help. Last time it didn't work at all, as you know."

"Can't you persuade Father Francis to be more patient?" asked Aunt Mary. "It seems to me that we don't need to push so hard. Eventually he will join all the other boys who go to the church regularly, and may become a Roman Catholic like them. After all, no Huguenots are left in the village to influence him anymore."

"I don't think you are right, Mary, for children of the Huguenots most often are more stubborn than their parents. But what is the good of talking when we just cannot do it. Father Francis insists that he must go to church at least twice a week. I saw him this afternoon and I am sure that he is watching us closely, hoping for an opportunity to get rid of the boy as soon as he can find an excuse to send him to a monastery. He knows that we have become attached to the boy, but he doesn't care about our feelings."

"But, Louis, you won't let Francis take him away, will you?" she protested indignantly. Uncle Louis shrugged his shoulders.

"What else can I do when the boy is so stubborn? He even makes it dangerous for us.[6] My objections may be a good excuse for Francis to send me to the galleys, too, just so that he can inherit this house, which is one of the few things he would like to have."

Tears came into Aunt Mary's eyes but she said nothing more and the meal was finished in silence.

A short time later, when Aunt Mary was clearing away the dishes, the kitchen door opened and John walked in. He was now a sturdy, sixteen-year-old boy who looked very healthy. Having lived nearly his whole life in the forest, he knew the animals and the plants that grew in the woods better than anyone else in the village. Usually, it was not very easy to intimidate him, but tonight he had a kind of timid, guilty look on his face. It was not that he was afraid of Uncle Louis, for he could easily endure a thrashing by him. It was well known that Uncle Louis was too big-hearted to give anyone a really painful beating. No, it wasn't Uncle Louis but the sad look on Aunt Mary's face that troubled John. He knew that she was worried and afraid of the consequences when he did not attend Mass. Today was the fifth time that he had played hookey from church, and he was sure that Aunt Mary and Uncle Louis knew it. There were always people to tell them.

Everybody seems to feel that they must keep an eye on me because I am a Huguenot, he thought bitterly.

He was somewhat surprised that the kitchen was so quiet, with Uncle Louis standing calmly close to the fireplace, busily engaged in sharpening a sliver of wood for cleaning his teeth. He had expected Uncle Louis to scold him, and Aunt Mary to be crying, but Uncle Louis looked up and just said, "Well, John, I heard that you didn't attend Mass this morning, and I feel that we must talk it over but first you must eat your supper."

The boy, surprised by this nice reception, looked uncertainly from his uncle to his aunt and back again, and wondered, did Uncle Louis mean it? Could he really eat his supper? Things seemed to be better than he had anticipated, and suddenly he realized how hungry he was.

---

[6] Anybody helping a Huguenot was treated as a Huguenot and could be punished with a life term on a galley.

"Come on, John," Aunt Mary said. "Hurry up a bit and sit down at the table. Aren't you hungry? I saved a large piece of meat for you."

Neither Uncle Louis nor Aunt Mary said anything during his meal, but when he was done, Uncle Louis, who was sitting in front of the fireplace, asked John to join him. Still wondering, the boy obeyed. Why weren't Uncle Louis and Aunt Mary angry?

All at once he became afraid. Had they made up their minds that they didn't want him anymore because he had been so disobedient? Were they going to send him away? Uneasy, he looked at his uncle's face, but it was too dark to see him clearly.

"Well, John, you didn't attend Mass today. Obviously it was on purpose. Why not?"

John didn't answer the simple question. What could he say? After all, Uncle Louis knew the reason as well as he, and he might become angry if he told him so again. He decided it was better to keep his mouth shut.

"No, John, don't be afraid to talk. You are old enough to understand that your refusal to go to the Mass puts us both in a very awkward and difficult position. Mind, I'm not angry with you. I know that you disobeyed because you don't see the situation in the proper light. Therefore, I want to talk with you as a grown-up and show you why your attitude is wrong. Tell me, why don't you go to church?"

John was embarrassed for he had only thought about his own troubles and had never realized it must be hard for his uncle and aunt, also.

Yet, they are willing to help me, he thought warmly. But how could he explain it to his uncle, who was a Roman Catholic?

It had grown dark in the kitchen. Aunt Mary who had finished cleaning the dishes, lit a candle and put it on the table.

In daylight John might have been embarrassed to tell what his mother had taught him but the dim light from the candle wasn't even enough to distinguish the other's faces, which made talking much easier.

"I can't go to the Roman Church, Uncle Louis, for Mother told me how wicked that church is. She said that it is impossible to go to it, and to follow Jesus at the same time. She warned me never to go, even when people are trying to force me for it is better to suffer the worst consequences than to disobey God. You know, Father was sent to the galleys for his faith, and he said that God will help me, and . . ."

John stopped, feeling that he would burst out in tears if he said more. Uncle Louis, seeing his grief, bent over and patted him on the knee.

"Well, John, we understand very well how you feel. Your father was my favorite brother, and you know that we, too, are sorry that he was sent away. For that very reason we are doing our utmost to keep you here. I don't know much about the Bible since I am not allowed to read it, but I remember that Father Francis once told me that the Bible teaches clearly that children must obey their parents. Nowadays Aunt Mary and I are taking the place of your parents and so I'm sure that you must obey us. What do you think about that?"

"But, Uncle Louis," John protested, "Mother told me that we always must obey God."

"Of course, John, but you must have misunderstood her. Isn't obeying God the same as obeying your parents, as the Bible teaches? Besides, it's also important for another reason. We haven't any children and would love to adopt you as our own son. When we are old we plan to give this house to you, and then you will be honored everywhere in the village! That is possible only if you go to church once in a while, and then everything will work out easily. And besides, you don't have to believe everything the priests tell you, anyway. I don't believe it all myself. And yet I always go to Mass because it's the only way to live peacefully in the village. For you it's even worse. If you don't attend Mass regularly, Father Francis will send you away. Although we would miss you very much, we wouldn't be able to stop him. Well, what more can I say? It's your duty to obey us and go to church, if only for our sake.

"You must also consider how much of an influence you may have in the village when you are grown up. Who knows? Everything may change in the future and you might be the only one left who is able to tell the people here about the Bible. What do you think? Isn't it far better to remain in the village and to be useful as an adult than to be brought up in a monastery? It doesn't help anybody when they force you to become a monk, does it?"

He waited a few moments and then continued, "It has been a tiring day for you and it is already late. Tomorrow I'll be going to the fair in St. Etienne, and will be back the day after. This is an excellent opportunity for you to consider what I've told you tonight. When I return, I hope to hear that you have decided to go to church. We may also try to bring back your little sister, Manette. Father

Francis can hardly refuse such a request if you attend Mass regularly for the time being. Now, off to bed. Good night, John."

It was far past midnight. John hadn't slept at all after having gone to bed in the attic. He tossed and turned restlessly from one side to the other, but sleep didn't come, in spite of everything he had tried. He had counted sheep until it bored him. Once he had thrown his blanket off, but a moment later he had crept deep underneath it again. He had lain on his stomach and his back. Nothing worked! He couldn't stop thinking and the more he thought, the more frightened and worried he became. The talk with Uncle Louis had convinced him that his staying away from church would make things very difficult. Something must be done about it, but he just didn't know what! True, he had two more days before Uncle Louis would be back, but that didn't help him now. He could not sleep!

It was stifling hot in bed. Again he threw his blanket off, resolutely jumped out of bed, and went to the window hoping it would cool him down enough to fall asleep later. The cool night breeze felt good on his face, and just looking at the friendly moon and stars gradually settled his excitement to a calm, thoughtful mood.

He had never seen the village at night, and was surprised how quiet and peaceful it looked. The bright moon made it possible to distinguish all the houses in the street. He could see the church and the house of Father Francis clearly and all those bitter memories returned again. He remembered that all their troubles had started four years ago with Father Francis telling the bishop that they were Huguenots. His father was sent to the galleys and had never been heard from again.

Two years later another dreadful event had occurred. Uncle Francis had invited Manette for lunch. Naturally, his mother didn't dare refuse, and so she had let his little sister go. That night, Uncle Francis himself had come to their cottage and told them that she had been sent to Paris to be brought up in the Roman Catholic religion by an old lady.[7] How his mother had cried! From that time on she slowly became weaker, and three weeks ago she had passed away.

Reliving these sad events brought tears in his eyes. He felt so very lonely, and he wished so much to talk with his mother, if only

---

[7] The law of 1686 decreed that all Huguenot children between five and sixteen years old must be taken away from their parents and given to Romanists or to monasteries to be brought up in the Roman Church.

for a moment. She would surely understand how dangerous his disobedience was. Maybe she wouldn't like his stubbornness, either, and would tell him to give in. After all, why shouldn't he do what Uncle Louis recommended? Going to the Roman Church was a small price, indeed, for living peacefully with his uncle and aunt. Besides, Uncle Louis was right. Nobody needed to know that he didn't believe the Romanist teachings. How nice it would be to have Manette with them again in a few years. Then he could also keep his promise to his father to take care of her.

Yet, his father and mother hadn't given in, and he knew why! He had promised Mother for that same reason never to go to the Roman Church and to read the Bible regularly. One night Mother and he had talked for a very long time. She had told him of the martyrs who had suffered for Christ's sake, singing Psalms while being burned at the stake. She had made it clear that everyone has to make a choice, either to live with Christ or to fight against Him. No other possibility existed. Living with Christ meant that all your sins were forgiven by His sacrifice on the cross. It also meant that you should never betray Him.

During their talk he had asked if there were any countries where it was possible to worship the Lord without the dangers they faced in France. His mother had sighed and mentioned Holland, a country far away where nobody was persecuted for serving the Lord. It was such a pity that they couldn't go there since the Huguenots were forbidden to take their children with them to another country. If his father and mother had gone to Holland, he and Manette would have been taken away, and sent to a cloister. They could only be patient and if need be, suffer for Christ's sake. In reality it was not as bad as it appeared because they were sure to live with Christ in heaven.

All at once he knew that, in spite of all his reasoning, he couldn't become a Roman Catholic. He wanted to belong to Christ like his parents and didn't want to deny Him. Yet, he was afraid to be sent to a monastery. He had heard enough stories to know how badly they treated boys like himself. They might lock him up in a tiny cell for the rest of his life, and even torture him. How could he escape such a dreadful life?

He was only a boy, and couldn't fight alone against all the priests! Thinking this, he lifted his head with a jerk for it suddenly dawned on him that this was not true. His thoughts were utter nonsense, for he didn't have to fight alone. Hadn't Mother told him that the Lord would never forsake His children? Hadn't she taught him to pray? He blushed for this very night he had completely forgotten his evening prayer. He hadn't told the Lord his difficulties and worries as he should have done before anything else.

Slowly, he left the window and before he went back to bed, he knelt on the floor and prayed. He prayed for his father and Manette but above all he asked the Lord to give him a brave and faithful heart so that he could resist all temptation and be a true servant of Jesus Christ. When at last he crept into his bed again, he was so calm and glad that in a very short time he fell asleep.

3

THE SECRET HIDING PLACE

Uncle Louis and Aunt Mary had only a few hours sleep that night. They were already working when the sun had barely risen above the horizon. Aunt Mary prepared breakfast and Uncle Louis went to the barn. He spread a heavy layer of straw into the wagon, and loaded a few pigs which he intended to sell at the market. After feeding the horse and harnessing it to the wagon, he tied it with a rope to the tree in front of the house.

"That's better," he said to the horse. "I wouldn't want you to run away without me. Now, be a good girl and wait for me while I eat something, for I'd rather not start this long trip on an empty stomach." He turned around, looked at the sky to see what the weather was likely going to be, and hurried inside.

"Mary," he called even before he was in the room. "Is breakfast ready? I must go as soon as possible for I don't want to be too late at the market. Even if I hurry, it will be at least noon before I get there since I've to drop Father Francis off at the bishop's palace first."

"Everything is ready, and I packed a good lunch for you," Aunt Mary replied. "What? You have to take Francis with you? You never told me!"

"Oh," Uncle Louis said carelessly, "yesterday I told him I was going to the market and he wanted very much to go with me to see the bishop for some reason."

His wife looked at him reflectively and said, "Maybe you could use this trip to convince him that he should be friendlier to John. You'll be sitting next to each other for several hours, and there is no better topic for discussion!"

Uncle Louis laughed. "Are you still fretting about John? Don't! Stop worrying! Last night I watched him closely and I'm quite sure that he understands perfectly well what I told him. He was impressed and seems to realize that he can't stay with us unless he becomes more reasonable. Do you know what you should do? Find some good excuse to send him to his home in the forest. It'll give him time to think and straighten things out in his mind. As a matter of fact, I am quite hopeful after last night that he can stay with us."

"Oh, I think so, too, but you had better make sure that Father Francis doesn't spoil everything!"

"Who cares about Francis? After awhile he will be sensible again, and if not, so what? But now I must leave. It is getting late."

They had eaten their breakfast during the conversation, and after kissing goodbye, Uncle Louis left. Aunt Mary listened to him climb on the wagon and tell the horse to giddyap. A few moments later she heard the crunching of the wheels on the road and then everything became quiet again. She remained standing a few more minutes, weighing Louis' words until suddenly a friendly smile brightened her face.

"Yes, that's what I'll do. I'll let John sleep and will do his morning chores. When he is awake, I'll tell him to go to his own house to pick the beans in the garden. It's pleasant work, and he needs some relaxing badly, the poor boy, for things are really hard for him lately."

Cheerfully she left the kitchen and went to the barn to milk the cows. There wasn't a reason in the world to feel depressed because Louis felt that everything would be alright with John.

A few hours later John woke up. Lazily he turned around and looked toward the radiant sunlight shining through the window, brightening the rather simple bedroom. He saw that it must be late, and sat up, amazed that he had slept so long. Why hadn't Aunt Mary called him, he wondered. He rose early every morning to help milk the two cows and fetch water and firewood. For a few moments he remained sitting and listened. He decided the milking must have been done already because he heard his aunt scouring the pots and the pans in the kitchen. Where could Uncle Louis be? Oh, yes, he remembered. Today he was going to the market and apparently had left early. Thinking about his uncle reminded him of last evening's discussion and his good intentions. He was sure now that he couldn't obey his uncle in this matter. As far as the consequences of his decision were concerned, he didn't dare to think about them, but planned to keep trusting the Lord, Who would surely help.

After a few moments, he jumped out of bed, dressed himself, and went to the kitchen where Aunt Mary was diligently cleaning the milkpails.

"Good morning, Lazybones," she said. "I do your work when you sleep late, as you can see." She pretended to be angry with him, but he saw her eyes twinkling mischievously.

"I really must teach you a lesson so that it won't happen again. Wait till you are through with breakfast then I'll punish you severely. But first wash yourself at the well. I don't like dirty faces."

John smiled and went to the door.

"Good morning, Auntie. It's your own fault. Why didn't you wake me up? You had no business doing my chores, anyway."

"Don't worry about it, Son. I've enough jobs left to keep you busy the rest of the day and longer. Better eat as much as you can for you will surely need it."

He wondered while he washed himself what kind of special chores she could have found for him. Maybe she wanted him to clean out the pigsty but that wasn't really anything special.

It didn't take long to eat several slices of bread with bacon, which Aunt Mary made while teasing him pitilessly about sleeping so long. As soon as he was ready, she went to the barn and returned with a large basket.

"Well, after having eaten so much, it's good to make up for it by working. I want you to go to your mother's garden and pick the beans. It would be wasteful not to eat them. Try to fill this basket up to the very brim. I've packed a good lunch for you to take along, and I don't want to see you before evening. Come on, slowpoke, hurry up before the day is over."

John, who was still sitting at the table, moved his chair vigorously and jumped up as if he would start working right away, but rather than grasping the basket he suddenly hugged his aunt.

"Isn't that an excellent idea. There is nothing that I'd like better in this beautiful weather."

"Stop it, impertinent good-for-nothing. Don't you know better than to kiss an old woman like me? Away with you, to the forest!"

With a quick movement, she freed herself from his arms, pushed him through the door, and threw the basket after him, laughing heartily.

"Oh, wait, John, I nearly forgot. Don't take other boys with you for they may damage the house and make sure that you are home again before dark. See you tonight! Bye."

After patting him on his shoulder, she closed the door behind him. He grasped the basket, put his arms through the leather straps that were attached to it and hoisted it onto his back. After crossing the street and some small patches of cultivated land, he had left the village and was on his way to his parent's home.

It was deliciously cool under the big trees in the forest. First he saw and heard many birds chirping to each other and singing their melodious songs, but as he went deeper into the woods the birds disappeared gradually. It was far easier for them to find their food at the edge of the woods, and so they disliked going deeper into it.

Often he saw the trails of the forest animals. Deer, foxes, and wild swine were very common, and the hares and rabbits were so abundant that they sometimes scampered away just before his feet. The forests, the villages, and all the surrounding country belonged to the Compte[8] de Mordiau, who spent nearly all his time far away in Paris, the capital of France. A steward looked after his very extensive property and at the Compte's order organized hunting parties once or twice a year. For that reason nobody but the Compte and the nobles, who hunted with him, were allowed to kill any animal. The deer, rabbits, and all the other animals multiplied quickly because the hunting parties were too few. As a result, the animals ate a great part of the crops grown by the farmers, who were poor because of both their small harvests and the very high taxes they paid to the Compte. John knew all these things, but didn't worry about them. He was far too happy to see all the familiar things of the forest again.

After an hour's walk he followed the familiar small trail, rarely used and completely overgrown with all kinds of plants.

There was so much to see that his firm step had already slowed down to an easy stroll. He couldn't help that his thoughts kept going back to his talk with Uncle Louis last evening. He wished that he could run away, but that was impossible without money!

At last he came to the small clearing in the woods from where he could see their old house, a simple cabin with small windows because his father could never afford larger window panes. Built against the back of the house was a little shed in which they had kept a goat. A small distance behind the shed was the pigsty. The house was surrounded by several fruit trees, the largest one in front, just next to the well. He remembered that his mother used to sit in its shade on hot days. Although the place made a desolate impression,

---

[8] Compte de Mordiau = The Count of Mordiau. The nobility and the clergy owned most of the country. The nobles spend nearly all their time in Versailles, at the court of the king. A steward was in charge of their estates. The country people were generally very poor because of the incredible high taxes levied by the nobility.

it was so familiar that it seemed to him as if his mother might at any moment walk out the door and say, "Hello, Son. Where have you been?" just as she used to do.

He went to the house, but remained standing outside a long time before he had the courage to enter, although the open door seemed to invite him to go in. Nobody could be there, of course, but once inside he looked around as if he expected to see somebody. Suddenly he realized far more clearly than before that he was alone. His mother, father, and Manette were gone and he wouldn't see them anymore! He became so sad that he let himself fall on the ground and burst out in tears. He felt so lonely for nobody in the whole world cared for him except, maybe, Uncle Louis and Aunt Mary, but they could never replace his own father and mother. Soon he stopped crying for he knew it didn't help. Nothing would change! Listlessly, he dried his tears and stood up. He knew he must begin picking the beans, and try to forget his grief. After all, his mother would never come back and he didn't know if he would ever see his father or sister again.

After he had taken the basket from his back, he put it on the ground and went to the garden. Yes, it was true. The plants were loaded with beans, just right for picking. Within a few hours, though, he could finish his chore. Feeling thirsty after his long walk, he went to the well for a drink. Fortunately, the pail for hauling the water up was still there, its chain attached to the well with a clamp. He dropped the pail into the water, pulled it up after it was filled, and grasping it with both his hands, drunk the refreshing water in large draughts. Did that ever taste good!

Still feeling uncomfortably hot and dry, he plunged his head into the half-full pail after having drunk his fill. It did help cool him down, but working in the kitchen garden while exposed to the burning sun was certainly nothing to look forward to. With a quick movement he stripped his shirt off and dropped it nonchalantly on the ground next to the basket.

"That feels better," he said to himself. "Let's begin with the job."

For a long time he picked beans diligently, and after a few hours of hard work he saw that he was doing fine. The basket was nearly full, and it wouldn't take more than another hour to fill it completely.

While resting for a moment, he realized suddenly that this was an excellent opportunity to look for the hiding place where his mother had kept the Bible. She had mentioned it during their last talk, urging him to live close to Christ. At last, she became tired. He had asked her to try to rest, but she had refused.

"It may be too late, then," she had said with a sweet smile on her face, and although she tried hard, she couldn't say much more. While she was telling him that a Bible was hidden behind a loose brick of the fireplace, she had begun to stammer and finally fell asleep, never to wake up again.

From that time on he had been so sad that he hadn't thought for a single moment about the Bible. It had been impossible to look for it in secret anyway. Both his uncles, Father Francis and Uncle Louis, had come after his mother's passing away, and had taken the few pieces of furniture his mother owned. Uncle Louis then took him home to live with him and Aunt Mary where he was still staying.

Now he could spend all day searching for the Bible without anybody noticing. What time was it? he wondered. He looked toward the sun and decided that it must be around noon. Another hour would be enough to fill the basket, and then he could use the rest of the afternoon to search for the Bible. He didn't know exactly where it was hidden but felt that it wouldn't be difficult to figure it out. Quickly he resumed the picking again, and soon the basket was filled to the brim.

"Fine, that will do," he said cheerfully, and walked to the well where he had put his lunch. The work had made him so hungry and thirsty that he ate with large mouthfuls, and in a short time he was ready for the search.

Still chewing his last mouthful, he entered the house, went to the fireplace, and scrutinized all the bricks. Yes, that must be it, he said to himself. One of the bricks appeared to be somewhat different from the rest. A closer look revealed that the joints around it were not filled with cement like the others. He took his knife which he always carried, put it in one of the joints and tried to lift the brick. After trying it a number of times, he had to give up. It didn't work. Every time he moved the brick the knife slid out of the joint without lifting it even slightly. There must be a better way to remove the brick, he thought.

Searching for a tool to move the brick, he looked around the empty room. He needed something that would fit into the joints at both sides of the brick, a kind of lever. He knew it would be impossible to remove the brick without such a tool for the joints were far too narrow for his fingers. Although there wasn't anything in the empty room, all at once he had an idea that he should look for something usable in the shed or the pigsty. He went outside and looked, but didn't find anything and went back to the house again.

Wait, he thought. I haven't checked the bed yet. The bed was built in the wall, and was partially filled with old straw. Nothing there! Underneath the bed was a small closet in which his mother used to keep odds and ends. He opened the small door, laid down on his stomach, and looked inside. At first it also seemed to be empty, but when his eyes became accustomed to the darkness, he saw something lying in the farthest corner. He couldn't see clearly what it was, and it was beyond his reach.

The closet opening was uncomfortably small, but by turning and pushing he managed to wrench his upper body deep enough into it so that he could grasp the object. The moment he had it in his hand he knew what it was, an old pair of fire tongs that his mother used for throwing wood on the fire. Well, who knows, he thought, maybe it will work if the jaws are flat enough.

He hurried back to the fireplace to try it out. Yes, the jaws of the fire tongs fitted easily into the joints. After closing them, he quickly pulled at the brick, but the sudden shock caused the brick to slip out of the jaws. He tried it again and being wiser now, was more cautious. Skillfully manipulating the fire tongs, he slid the brick slowly from the chimney wall and dropped it carelessly to the floor. Looking into the opening, he saw a piece of cloth, and after throwing it impatiently aside, the Bible!

It stood on its end, leaning against the wall of the hole. It was much larger than John had expected. Apparently, the old rag had protected the Bible from being damaged by the rough brick bottom. He lifted the Bible carefully from the hole, and saw, to his great surprise, another smaller package in the corner, also wrapped in a piece of cloth. It was small and hard. Apparently, it had been in the hole a long time because the piece of linen wrapped around it was dirty and yellowed.

Slowly, he unwrapped the parcel until, suddenly, something fell on the ground with a barely audible, musical sound. He was amazed to see a thin necklace with a kind of cross and a coin dangling at the end of it. Where did this thing come from? he wondered. His mother had never worn jewelry because they had been too poor to buy such luxuries. He picked the coin from the floor and examined it closely

Both sides of the coin had a picture, somewhat worn out but still distinctive. One side showed an open Bible underneath a heart, with a few words written in it. His sharp eyesight and the bright sunlight made it possible to read the words, "Fear not, little flock. Luke 12:32."

It was a passage from the Bible that he knew. It made a great impression on him for it seemed that these words were written especially for him. How strange! The very moment that he was scared and needed encouragement badly, the Lord told him not to be afraid because He would help him. All at once he also remembered another passage that his mother had told him to memorize, "And by my God I have leapt over a wall." If God helped, why should he be afraid?

He turned the coin around to look at the picture on the other side. It was of a Shepherd with a tiny herd. The Shepherd was armed with a spear and blew a trumpet to warn the sheep of approaching danger. Obviously, the Shepherd was Christ, Who gathered His Church and protected His flock against the wickedness of the world.

Looking at this medal, he remembered vaguely that his father had talked about the coins used by the Huguenots to recognize each other so that no traitor could enter their meetings. He didn't know if they still were being used. The Huguenot cross which he examined next was familiar to him. His father used to wear it secretly and must have placed it in the hiding place after their visit to Father Francis. Resolutely he hung the necklace around his neck and hid the coin and the cross underneath his clothing. After all, he thought, I am also a Huguenot and the necklace is a beautiful remembrance.

He still had the rest of the parcel in his hand, and now continued to unwrap it, wondering if it contained anything else. Yes, he saw a yellow coin, a piece of gold! He had never seen such a coin before but knew that it was money, a real gold coin called a Louis d'Or after the image of the king who was pictured on it. It was quite a lot of money for a simple boy like him. It would even have been a lot of money for his father. He wondered how his parents had gotten it.

He couldn't have known that his mother had put aside every cent she could save for years and years to get this gold piece. She had intended to use the money to buy a Bible for the children when they were old enough. Although she couldn't save any longer after her husband was sent to the galleys, she hadn't touched her little treasure in the hiding place.

John shrugged his shoulders. What could he do with the money? He couldn't give it to Uncle Louis because he would ask about the hiding place.

He picked one of the rags from the ground and wrapped the coin again. Then a sudden thought struck him. Could it be an answer to his prayers? Maybe he could use the money to run away if they tried to send him to a monastery. However, he might not have the chance to get the money out of the hiding place when that happened so he decided to take it with him and hide it at his uncle's place so that he would have it handy when he needed it. But . . . why wait so long? Why not run away now?

This thought was such a great surprise to him that he needed to think it over quietly. He went outside and sat down in the shadow of the old apple tree to consider all the possibilities. Suppose finding the coin was an answer to his prayers, and he didn't use it. To leave now was very attractive but not very smart, everything considered. He knew that he had to walk north to reach Holland, but what should he do to make certain that he wasn't caught? That was the most difficult problem he faced.

Gradually his thoughts began to straighten themselves out and he worked out a plan that he thought might succeed. He wouldn't take the regular roads, but would go through the forest, which he knew well. Sure, it meant that instead of going north, he would go west, but so what? Nobody would search for him in that direction and later he could turn north.

For the first few days, though, he knew he must hide somewhere in the neighborhood until they had stopped searching for him. Then he could go through the woods without danger of being caught. But where could he hide so that he wouldn't be found? Well, he knew several hiding places and one of them was ideally suited. Twenty minutes walk from their cottage was a large clearing in the woods, completely filled with thistles, nettles, and wild rosebushes. It was nearly impossible to go through it, even when wearing high hip boots, without being scratched all over. He would need a sharp axe to cut a path for himself. Nearly in the center of the clearing was a small open place he had discovered some time ago, while chasing a rabbit. The animal had jumped into a dry ditch covered over with bushes. He had followed the rabbit on his belly, and discovered that open space.

He was still sitting on the ground, leaning against the wall of the cottage, when he saw to his dismay that the sun was already setting. Naturally, it was impossible to leave tonight without preparing for his flight. No, tomorrow night he could be ready! In the meantime there was no need to carry his newly found treasures with him, and so he returned everything to the secret enclosure, replaced the brick, and removed all visible traces of the opening. Then, he hoisted the basket on his back and hurried home to Aunt Mary.

4

THE ESCAPE

The next day John was very tired when he came home for supper. All morning he had worked hard for Aunt Mary and in the afternoon had returned to his parent's home where he had also been busy.

It had been impossible to sneak away during the morning chores because Aunt Mary had stayed with him the whole time. Before her usual nap after lunch, however, she had given him permission to spent the rest of the afternoon with the other boys, provided he was home early enough to clean out the chicken coop. Happy that she didn't need him anymore, he had gone directly to the cottage and prepared his hiding place to run away.

First, he enlarged the open space in the thornbushes using only his knife, which was rather difficult and time consuming. Next, he had gathered pine needles and moss to be used as a bed. Unfortunately, he had nothing to carry them in, and so he used his shirt as a kind of bag, which he dragged behind him as he crawled on his stomach through the narrow, dry ditch. It took many trips before the pile was large enough for ample bedding, and the sun was already setting when he was more or less ready with everything he had planned. He didn't like the idea that Aunt Mary would be cross with him again for walking in after suppertime and for a moment he considered not going back. After all, he planned to run away that very same night, anyway. Yet, it wouldn't be so smart not to go home this last night, for it was important to have at least a three-day supply of food. Besides, he also needed a small axe to cut down a rosebush to conceal the entrance to his hiding place. No, it was better to go home. He might change his mind, though, if Uncle Louis had already returned because he was afraid that he would inadvertently give his plans away to Uncle Louis, who couldn't be easily fooled.

Happily, the stable was empty when he arrived. Uncle Louis hadn't returned yet. With a kind of guilty feeling he entered the house, but had barely crossed the doorstep when Aunt Mary began to scold him. She wasn't nearly as angry as she pretended, for in her heart she was glad to see him even though he was late. She was somewhat disappointed, though, that he had left her at home alone while Uncle Louis was gone.

"Where have you been? I tried to find you all afternoon but nobody knew where you were. Where did you go? Come on, tell me right away."

John did not know what to say, and was smart enough to hold his tongue.

"Don't stand there like a fool. Tell me what you did this afternoon. You haven't lost your tongue, I hope?"

Still John didn't reply, but when he saw that Aunt Mary was waiting for some answer he shrugged his shoulders and said, "Oh, I just walked around."

This unreasonable answer made Aunt Mary really angry.

"Just walking around! What do you mean, eh? Are you trying to fool me? Where did you walk around, and why didn't anybody see you?"

She waited a few moments, but when John remained quiet she must have realized that he didn't want to tell her, and so she drew herself up and said, "John, go directly to bed. I have no supper for you. Disobedient boys do not deserve supper. I didn't expect such an attitude from you. As soon as Uncle Louis is home I'll tell him everything, and he'll punish you."

Slowly John went upstairs. What a pity that Aunt Mary was so angry. She and Uncle Louis had always been kind to him and his mother. After his father had been jailed, Uncle Louis had visited them often and after each visit he had left something, a piece of meat, some flour, or a piece of cloth. Thinking of their friendliness made him feel downhearted. For the first time it dawned on him that he would probably never see them again. Would they understand why he had run away? He wondered if he would ever be able to tell them. Maybe he could send a letter from Holland. Why not? This thought comforted and encouraged him a little.

It wasn't late yet and it would take many more hours before he could leave. He had to wait for Uncle Louis to come home, and even then he couldn't escape unless Uncle Louis and Aunt Mary were asleep. In the meantime, he must stay awake. If he fell asleep, he might not wake up in time and then his beautiful plan would fail miserably. It wasn't easy to stay awake because he couldn't walk around. Even sitting on the edge of his bed wasn't safe. Suppose that Aunt Mary would come upstairs unexpectedly and asked why he wasn't asleep in bed.

Yes, he had to go to bed, but must make sure that he didn't fall asleep and that was difficult. The first ten minutes or so it was rather easy to stay awake. He carefully went over his plans a few times, and made sure that he knew exactly what to take with him. Gradually however he became more and more drowsy. The whole long day he had worked hard outside in the open air, making him so tired that the bed felt more comfortable than ever. He struggled with that sleepy feeling by keeping his eyes wide open and listening for the arrival of Uncle Louis. Yet, his eyes became heavier and heavier, and after a short while he fell asleep and didn't even wake up when Uncle Louis returned home with the horse and wagon.

Downstairs, Aunt Mary was waiting for Uncle Louis. The single candle she had lit didn't give enough light for anything, but it made no difference to her. She was busy knitting, her usual pastime at night because she could do it even in the dark.

It takes Louis a long time to come home tonight, she thought. Usually, she did not mind being home alone, but today was different because she had so much to think about. Again and again her thoughts turned toward John and how they could keep him out of the hands of Father Francis. In her heart she wasn't certain that John would become Roman Catholic, in spite of Louis' encouraging words. After all, nobody could deny that his parents were Huguenots, and she knew the family of her husband well. All the men, without exception, were extremely stubborn. Not only John's father but also Louis and Father Francis, especially when they were convinced that they were right. John won't even consider the possibility of becoming Roman Catholic if he resembled his father in the slightest degree, she thought. Louis was by far too optimistic and would never be able to protect him. She considered briefly sending John to another part of the country where nobody knew him. She still had several cousins far away where he might stay. She decided to discuss it with Louis when he came home. In this manner she had been thinking and worrying the whole evening until suddenly she decided to try to take her mind off all her troubles.

"No, Mary," she told herself, "Worrying won't help. It is better to pray a rosary[9] for the benefit of the boy and the safe arrival of Louis."

She fumbled in the pocket of her skirt for her rosary, but before she had it ready she heard the trotting of a horse and the grinding of wagon wheels. Uncle Louis had arrived.

Quickly she stood up to prepare a cold supper. She put a piece of ham and a cold chicken on the table with a few slices of bread and a glass of wine. She heard Louis unharness the horse and bring it to the stable. He was in an ugly mood for he was making far more noise than usual and kicked the stable door shut with such a loud bang that the whole house vibrated. When he entered, she saw at once that something serious must have happened. Louis was usually calm and somewhat placid, but this night he was as furious as she had ever seen him!

"What's the matter, Louis? What has happened?" she asked anxiously.

He looked at her, still seething with rage, and said, "We are going to lose John. Father Francis, that pious hypocrite, has taken us for a ride."

"Oh, no, Louis, that's impossible. He never mentioned anything about it before."

"That is what we both thought. Today he promised the bishop that John will work in the palace and help the gardener. At night, he must sleep in the cloister, for they have plans to make a monk of him," Louis said bitterly. He let himself fall down on a chair, and pounded the table with his fist. "Fool that I am, I had to promise the bishop that John will be brought to his palace within ten days."

"But, Louis," said Aunt Mary, dazed, "You can't do that! No way! It's just impossible. You don't like it either, right? Let's help him to escape! We must keep John out of their paws! Come on, let's do something."

"No, Mary, I don't know what. All the way home, I tried to think of a way out, but I didn't come up with anything."

"Oh, you are tired. First eat and drink something. That helps a lot, and I am sure that you'll get some idea of how to help him."

---

[9] A rosary is a string of beads used to keep count when saying prayers. It contains five or fifteen sets consisting of one large bead and ten small beads. For each set the user says the Lord's prayer, followed by ten Hail Mary's and one Glory be to the Father. The rosary, used for many centuries in the Roman Catholic Church, is based on the unbiblical idolatry of Mary.

"Yes, I'd like to eat first, for I haven't had a thing since this morning."

She waited until he began to eat and then said slowly, "I was just thinking tonight that it will be impossible to keep John here, anyway. It is far better to send him secretly away to my family. I'm sure that my brother is willing to take him, especially because John has a pair of strong hands, and would be a good helper for his farm. He could come back to us within a few years when Father Francis has quieted down somewhat."

"Impossible, Mary. We must send the boy to the bishop. Listen to what has happened and you'll agree with me.

"Yesterday, I sold the pigs at the market and was ready to go home but Father Francis had not yet concluded his business. Anyway, it was too late to start home and so we stayed in the city, Francis in the cloister and I in the inn at the corner of the main street. This morning around eight o'clock I was ready to leave and drove to the monastery to pick up Francis. I waited for him at the gate, as we had agreed upon last night, but he didn't come out. A message boy came and told me that the bishop wanted to see me. Obviously, I didn't have the foggiest idea of why he wanted to talk to me. I assumed that he wanted to buy some grain or vegetables for the palace.

"When I entered his study, the bishop was talking with Francis but interrupted his conversation abruptly. He didn't even give me the opportunity to greet him. He turned abruptly toward me and said that Francis had told him that we were taking care of John, the son of Huguenot parents. He put a feather in our cap because he said we had practiced Christian hospitality, but he added that the church didn't like such a burden on our shoulders. He said his gardener needs a helper and it would be good for the boy to take that job. He mentioned that John would get a good Roman Catholic education and would receive excellent spiritual guidance, especially because he could stay at the cloister at night. 'If everything works out well,' he added, 'John might later decide to become a monk!'

"Naturally, I told him respectfully that John was no burden for us at all, that we loved him, that he seemed to feel at home helping us with the chores, and that we would rather bring him up ourselves, him being my own brother's boy. The bishop didn't pay any attention to my words and just repeated what he had already said. When I realized that he wasn't in the least interested in our feelings and wouldn't change his mind about John, I became furious and yelled that it was a dirty trick for Francis to hand John over to the bishop behind our backs. Well, that apparently was a bit too much for the bishop to swallow, for he gave me a tongue-lashing and asked Francis if I always behaved as a true, faithful Roman Catholic or if I also was contaminated by the Huguenots. I saw that Francis didn't like the insinuation. He hastened to assure the bishop that nothing was wrong with me but that I was attached to the boy and spoke rashly and insolently, being only an ignorant farmer without manners. The bishop appeared to be satisfied but he told me to pray fifty chaplets[10] as a punishment for my behavior. He added that he expected me to bring John within the next ten days and then dismissed us to go home. As you see, Francis has got me over the barrel again. If I don't bring John to the bishop I will be known as a Huguenot sympathizer or worse. There is no way out. I have to bring him no matter how badly we feel about it."

Aunt Mary had listened quietly to his story with tears glistening in her eyes. When he had finished she broke down and sobbed, "Louis, you can't do it. He will be dead and buried in no time when they force him to live in a monastery. He, an outdoor boy! You know as well as I that he will never become Roman Catholic and for that reason he will really be abused. We must find a way to help. Send him abroad if you think that living with my family isn't safe enough."

"No, Mary, I'm sorry but it can't be done. They would blame us and what would happen then? I don't want to be sent to the galleys for his sake, and I'm sure that you wouldn't like to be chased away from this place, either.[11] As a matter of fact, Francis would most likely be very pleased if that happened for then he would get our house. Nothing can be done! I've thought all day long but it is far too dangerous to obstruct the bishop's order. Maybe it won't be as bad for John as we think it will be. Anyhow, it's no use talking more about it. It's late. Let's go to bed."

Aunt Mary, still sobbing, said no more. Somewhat later, while Uncle Louis was undressing for bed, she cleaned away the dishes from the table and placed them in the cupboard. Once finished, she put a sizeable piece of cold chicken and a few slices of bread on a plate, intending to take it to John's bedroom upstairs. However, Uncle Louis interfered.

---

[10] A chaplet is a string of prayer beads one third the length of a rosary.

[11] The law of 1687 decreed that anyone who helped a Huguenot flee from France must receive capital punishment (death by hanging).

"What are you doing?" he asked, surprised.

"Well," she replied, "I'm going to take some food to John. He came home late tonight and I sent him to bed without supper. Now that the poor boy is going away, I don't like the idea that on one of his last nights at home he has to go to sleep with an empty stomach. The least I can do is take him a chicken leg."

Uncle Louis stood up, looked searchingly at her face, and said, "No, Mary, that won't do. You can't tell the boy what is going on. He would be a great fool not to run away. Even if you don't tell him, he may become suspicious seeing the tears on your face. It is better that I take the tray myself. Watch yourself tomorrow, too. Don't let him suspect anything! I am not kidding. It's really very dangerous for us if he escapes."

He took the tray out of Aunt Mary's hands, tiptoed upstairs, and found John sleeping as solid as a log. For a long time he stood looking down on him, sick at heart that he couldn't do anything to stop the bishop's plan. At last, he put the tray on the floor in front of the bed and shook his head.

"Poor boy," he muttered. "If I only had the power to help you. But it can't be done. It's impossible."

Very carefully, he caressed John's cheek with the back of his hand before he went downstairs again.

"It is outrageous to do such a thing to a mere boy only because his father is a Huguenot!"

John was dreaming. He was running as fast as possible through the forest. Behind him, Father Francis was running to catch him, and after him a whole crowd of people were running, all trying their best to get their hands on him. Every time when they grabbed him, he managed to tear himself loose and keep running and running. Suddenly a very wide ditch made it impossible to continue. In his terrible fear, he panicked and tried to jump across it but missed the other side and fell down into the water. He kept falling and falling and falling until everything became black behind him. The yelling and the noise of running feet of the mob became softer and softer and eventually he didn't hear anything. Suddenly he became alert. Somebody was calling him from far away. At first he didn't know who that could be, but after a few moments he realized with a shock that it was Manette's voice. Oh, yes, there she was, and she kissed him carefully on his cheek.

At that moment he woke up wondering what had happened. Had someone really kissed him or was he still dreaming? Nonsense, who would kiss him at night? But who was going down the stairs?

Still half asleep he sat up, and looked around. The moon shed a pale light through the window, illuminating the attic alcove somewhat. In front of his bed he saw a tray of food on the floor.

Oh, Aunt Mary must have brought up my supper, he thought. How nice she is. Maybe she is sorry that she has been so cross with me.

Wait a moment, he thought suddenly. He nearly had forgotten that he was planning to run away. He wondered what time it was and whether his uncle had come home yet.

He listened and he heard Uncle Louis' voice downstairs and a few whispered words by Aunt Mary. They hadn't gone to bed yet, and he had enough time to make everything ready. Afraid to fall asleep again, he put his legs outside the bed, and went quietly toward the window and sat down. Some time later Uncle Louis and Aunt Mary went to bed, but he continued to wait much longer until he felt it was safe enough to go.

He first tiptoed to the plate with chicken, for he was hungry, but changed his mind and decided not to eat. It would be better to take it with him. During the first few days of his flight he needed all the food he could get. He realized then that he needed some type of bag for carrying his few possessions and food. He wondered if he could find something useful in the pile of rags and worn-out clothes that were stored behind the attic door.

Quietly he moved toward the door but stopped after the first careful steps. How loudly the floor squeaked! He stood and waited with a pounding heart for a long time before he dared to move again. After a while, when he was sure they were still asleep downstairs, since everything remained quiet he slowly took a few more steps. He came close to the door, and opened it cautiously inch by inch to prevent it from squeaking. At first nothing happened, but suddenly it squeaked so loudly that he felt the noise in the marrow of his bones. At the same time, somebody downstairs turned around in his bed. For many minutes he remained standing still, not daring to move for fear that his uncle or aunt would wake up.

At last he gathered enough courage to open the door wider. Just one more step was needed to be close to the pile of rags. He couldn't see anything in the dark corner of the attic, just grabbed as much as he could carry in both his hands and quietly tiptoed back to his room. Close to the window, in the bright moonlight, he examined his catch. Most of the rags and clothes were absolutely useless, but one particular piece appeared to be exactly what he was looking for. It was one of his uncle's old shirts with several large holes in it. It was surely big enough, and the holes didn't matter too much — he could close them with a thin rope. It would be easy to convert the shirt into a bag by tying the sleeves and the collar.

During another tense trip across the attic he found a piece of rope, and after that it was just a matter of minutes before he had a kind of bag, which he filled with all the things he needed, and then he put the chicken on top.

Oh, yes, I almost forgot the blanket, he thought. He made a roll out of it and was ready to go.

He looked around his little room for the last time. Suddenly he became scared and thought, Isn't it foolish that a mere boy like myself hopes to escape all the dangers that lay ahead of me? Won't I be caught within a few days?

Yet he didn't hesitate. He knew that only with God's help could he hope to reach his destination.

The next moment he knelt spontaneously on the floor, and prayed to the Lord asking for guidance and protection on his dangerous flight. He also prayed to God to protect Manette and his father, and to bring them all together again. Finally, he asked for strength and perseverance during his flight, and the strength to never deny his Savior Jesus Christ, not even if caught.

After praying, John stood up and picked up his improvised bag and blanket. The two bundles were rather large and awkward to handle and he realized that it would be difficult to go through the house carrying them without making any noise. They might scrape against the wall or hit a piece of furniture, which might wake his uncle or aunt. He glanced through the room and quickly found a good solution. He went to the window, rolled the bag tightly inside the blanket, aimed and then threw it as far as possible onto the deserted village street. The parcel swirled through the air and hit the ground a fair distance from the house. The only sound was a soft thud and then everything was quiet again. It is an excellent beginning, he thought.

The next thing was to go through the house and get himself out, which wasn't easy. However, he had no choice because he had to get some food from the cupboard where Aunt Mary kept it. It was fortunate that she had baked bread just yesterday, so there were at least six loaves of bread. Two loaves would be enough for him, he figured, especially since he also had the vegetables from the garden and the chicken. For a fleeting moment he wondered if taking the loaves was stealing but convinced himself easily enough that it wasn't really theft. Aunt Mary would have given them gladly if she had known how badly he needed them.

After having stealthily tiptoed into the kitchen, he listened but heard nothing unusual in the bedroom where his uncle and aunt slept. Feeling his way around, he came to the closet and had just grasped its knob when somebody turned over in bed. A moment later Uncle Louis began to snore, which he always did when he was sleeping soundly. Everything appeared to be safe, but he waited a few more minutes to be certain before opening the door of the cupboard. Feeling around in it he found the two loaves of bread rather quickly. Without closing the cupboard door, he walked to the kitchen door, which was never locked. A few moments later he stood outside.

He waited a few minutes to make sure that everything was alright. Happily, everything remained quiet and it seemed to be safe. The walk to the hiding place would be child's play but before going on his way to the forest he went to the barn to fetch a small axe. The day before he had used it to cut some wood so he knew exactly where it was. With the axe in his hand, he went to the blanket parcel, laid it on his shoulder and was ready!

The street was deserted but still it seemed safer to leave the street as fast as possible. He crossed the road and carefully picked his way through the yard of the house across the street. Then he climbed over a few fences, went across a pasture, and after another ten minutes was walking happily through the forest along the paths he knew well.

5

EXCITEMENT IN THE VILLAGE

The next morning the village main street looked completely different than on other mornings. Usually it was quiet around ten o'clock. The men were working in the fields, and the women were inside cleaning up their houses. Small children usually played in the street, and the older boys and girls either helped their fathers and mothers or went to the little schoolhouse where the sexton taught them reading, writing, and arithmetic. The sexton barely knew these things himself and could not teach much, but that was fairly common in a small village so nobody felt it to be a disadvantage.

Today, everything was different. Nearly all the village women were standing together in small groups, talking fervently to each other. The little children were crawling and playing everywhere, and opposite the house of John's Uncle Louis a group of grown-up boys were arguing with loud voices and wild gestures. Everybody seemed excited and apparently no one had stayed indoors, except for a few old grandfathers who were too weak to work, and sat nonchalantly against the wall of a house. The only persons missing were the men.

The boys made the loudest noise. They all talked at the same time and every one of them tried to outscream the others.

"I can't see why everyone makes such a fuss because John ran away," shouted Antoine. "My father wouldn't mind at all if I disappeared. He would wait quietly until I came back and then would give me such a thrashing that I wouldn't dare to run away for the rest of my life."

"No, that isn't true at all," yelled another. "Your father would be glad if you ran away and never came back. 'Good riddance,' he would say. Your trouble is that you eat too much and do too little."

All the boys grinned for they all knew that nobody in the village was as lazy as Antoine, who liked nothing better than eating. None of the boys was as fat as he!

"I know why they are going after him," little Pierre, the son of the baker, remarked loudly. "He is kin to Father Francis, who can command everybody to search for him. Nobody would be interested in us if we disappeared."

"Nonsense," said Philippe, a farmer's boy. "The sexton told my father this morning that John was going to be sent to a monastery. They want him to become a good Roman Catholic and that is why they are so busy searching. After all, he is a Huguenot who has to be converted!"

"I don't know," another boy gave as his opinion, "it seems so silly to run away. No doubt they'll catch him and then he'll be far worse off. It would have been smarter to stay home with his uncle."

"Oh no," laughed Charles. "It's not as silly as you think. Now we have an extra day off, which I intend to enjoy thoroughly. You know what's silly? To remain hanging around here. Come on, stop wasting our time by gossiping like old women. Who will go with me to the churchyard to play hide and seek?"

A few seconds later all the boys had disappeared except little Pierre. His mother got hold of him just when he tried to sneak away without having done his usual morning chore of bringing firewood into the bakery. She had to bake the bread today instead of his father, who was lending a hand in the search.

However, all the other women kept talking. No one was in a hurry to begin their work including the wife of the baker.

"It's a shame," she said. "All the men ordered to search the roads and the woods just because Father Francis' naughty nephew has run away. Today, no work whatsoever will be done in the fields. It couldn't have happened at a worse time, either, right in the middle of the harvest when we need all hands available. Father Francis should be more concerned with how hard we work to make a living than with a runaway. I'm wondering how we will ever get the hay dry in the barn if it starts raining tomorrow. I bet that the boy will turn up within a few days, anyway. After all, he has no place to go. What else can he do?"

"I doubt it," the wife of the miller said. "I've known his father since we were small children. He always worked hard and was never drunk, not even during the holidays. His wife was nice and an example for everybody. I dare say that there was no better family around here. They were extremely stubborn, though, when it came to religion.

I wouldn't be surprised if the boy is like them and would rather starve than come back and eat crow."

"You are right, Rachel," another woman agreed. "I think that more is going on than Father Francis is willing to admit. I don't know what his intentions are, but the way he deals with his brother's family is scandalous. The father to the galleys, the girl to Paris, the mother dead of sorrow, and now he is after the boy. I think that John is far better off on his own than staying here. How miserable he would be if he had to live with his Uncle Francis as his guardian, never being sure if he wouldn't be sent away to a monastery someday."

Several faces turned pale upon hearing these bold words concerning Father Francis, and many looked with fear toward the wife of the sexton, who stood nearby! She was a fanatical churchgoer who literally worshipped the priest. Indeed, it didn't take long for her to reply.

"I warn you, Therese," she shouted in a shrill voice, her face red with anger. "I warn you to talk better of Father Francis. He is a pious man, willing to sacrifice everything for the church. You sound as if you are also contaminated with the poison of the Huguenots. Mind, they are good-for-nothings. Every one of them! You know as well as the rest of us that Father Francis is bending over backwards to help that boy. After lots of trouble he finally finds an excellent job for him in the garden of the bishop and what does he get? Thanks? No, the stripling doesn't like an honest day's work and runs away. It is always the same with those heretics. If you try to help them they give you dirt to eat. They are an ungrateful lot, always quarreling! They think that they know even more about the church than our beloved Father Francis, who studied such a long time. But I tell you, one of these days I'll tell him how you slander him and that you talk as a heretic. Then you'll see how he will treat you. He won't give you the holy sacraments anymore, and you'll go to hell like all heretics. That's exactly what you deserve, gossiping about our beloved priest."

Before she had finished, the other woman put her hands on her hips and said with contempt, stressing every word, "You don't need to yell, Barbara. I'm not deaf. I'll tell you something. I'm as good a Roman Catholic as you. Yet, I claim that Father Francis isn't as saintly as you think. The only thing he worries about is 'his' church but only because he makes a living of it. He tries hard to befriend the bishop to get a better position, and for that reason only is willing to sacrifice everything. As far as I'm concerned, we need him badly because he is a priest who can serve the Mass, but I have no use for him otherwise. And you are going to tell him that? I dare you to play the informer, Barbara. Try it and see what happens. I don't like dirty hands but you can be assured that my nails will scratch the dirt from your face if you are tempted to tell him what we, decent women, talk about. And now you'd better go home before I lose my temper completely."

At the same time she made some menacing steps into the direction of the sexton's wife who hurriedly retreated from the small group, afraid that sturdy Therese would really do what she said. She was boiling with rage and would have loved to seek revenge, but knew that it would be unwise to tell Father Francis anything. In general, Therese never said much but when she talked in this manner, you could be sure she would keep her word.

The only woman who didn't appear in the street was Aunt Mary. She stayed inside and kept herself busy with washing some clothes, but her thoughts kept turning to all the events that had taken place that morning. It had been rather late when she awoke, because her talk with Uncle Louis had kept her awake many hours worrying about John. The first thing she did was to call for him, standing at the bottom of the stairs. When he did not answer she assumed that he was already at work in the barn. She dressed quickly and hurried out to help him milk the cows.

But she didn't see him in the barn, and the cows hadn't been milked and fed. Suddenly she became suspicious and went to his little room in the attic. The mess he had left behind convinced her immediately that he had fled. At first she was disappointed, for she had secretly hoped that he would have stayed for her sake, but right away her common sense told her that his escape was far better. She knew now that Francis had planned to send him away to the bishop, and that Louis was unable to protect him. But, she thought quickly, what will happen to me and Louis now? Will we also be sent to prison?

She had hurried downstairs and awakened Louis. When he heard the news he leaped out of bed and hurried to John's little room. Yes, it was true. John was gone. Louis had been frightened and angry, but calmed down after a remarkably short time and even said that deep in his heart he would be glad if John's flight were successful, provided it would not be so dangerous for them.

They knew it was most important to convince Father Francis that they had not helped the boy. Immediately, without even considering breakfast, Louis had gone to the house of his brother and told him everything about John's flight.

After his return he told Mary that matters were not as bad as they had expected. Francis and he had quarreled, but his brother was willing to help for his own sake. After all, it would be a large blot on his own name if his whole family was sent to the galleys for their Huguenot inclinations. He had sent the sexton down to the village to call all the men together in the church, where he had commanded them to search the roads and the woods. Next, he wrote letters to the priests in the neighboring villages requesting them to keep an eye on the roads. These letters were delivered by some farmers who owned horses. They had agreed not to send any message to the bishop, at least not yet. Maybe the boy would be caught within the next two or three days and if not, it was still early enough to inform the bishop that he had fled without any help from outsiders.

Thinking this over, Aunt Mary smiled a little. She was glad that everything seemed to be turning out all right. She didn't have to worry about Louis' safety, and she hoped that John was able to outwit his searchers.

That night she went to bed with a mixture of strange feelings. Happily, the searchers had found no trace of John, but she felt sad that he was gone.

"It will be quiet again in the house," she thought and tried to comfort herself by thinking of Manette.

"Maybe we can get her back in a few years when all the trouble with John is forgotten." She knew that it was most unlikely but she tried to keep thinking about Manette to overcome the aching she felt deep in her heart.

Father Francis went to bed late that night. All the men had returned without finding any trace of John. Where could he be? he thought. It was impossible to have walked very far in one day. He decided that the men had to continue the search tomorrow. John must be found. If not, his relationship with the bishop, which had improved so much lately, would again be in jeopardy, and it would be John's fault. He hated John and his whole family. Now they would be a stumbling block for his next promotion. First the father, now the son. How was it possible to advance with such a family in the village! Yet, that wasn't the only reason why he had delivered his brother into the hands of the Inquisition. No, he hated his brother thoroughly for telling him that he was a bad priest and wasn't preaching the true word of God. He clenched his fists. He wished that he could destroy that whole family!

6

HAIR RAISING EXPERIENCES

It was an extremely hot day. The unrelenting sun had scorched the forest continuously so that it was impossible to find any cool spot in the afternoon. Most of the grass had turned into a sickly yellow-brown and the trees had lost their nice fresh green colors. Even the rabbits and the foxes and all the other animals were not to be seen. They had gone into their dens to stay until the sun had lost its greatest intensity. Then they could go out foraging again. Only the bees, wasps, mosquitos, and butterflies did not seem to be bothered by the high temperature, for they flew happily around as if the burning sun had given them an extra dose of strength.

John was sleeping quietly in his hiding place. Two days ago he had left his uncle's house, and he had been very busy in arranging everything he needed for survival, especially the first night. Obviously, having a sufficient supply of water was of the utmost importance for it would be nearly impossible to stay in hiding without it. The well of the cottage was close by, and he counted on using the pail to carry the water.

He had not expected that it would be so difficult to loosen the bucket from the chain that connected it to the well. First he had tried to open one of the chainlinks by hammering it flat with a stone, and bruised two fingers when he hit them by mistake. When the worst pain had lessened, he had tried it again with his knife, but that hadn't worked either. At last he managed to loosen the pail handle on one side by forcing his axe between the handle and the pail itself. He now had the opportunity to use the pail with or without the chain. After that was done, he hadn't expected any trouble in getting water from the well and carrying it. How wrong he had been! So much time had been lost by removing the chain that the night was nearly gone and the sky was beginning to become lighter, which made him hurry back to the safety of his hiding place with a pail of water. Running without spilling water is an art in which he wasn't very skilled, as he soon found out, for he arrived at his hideout with a pair of wet feet and a pail only half-filled with water.

Next, he quickly cut down a large, wild rosebush, and dragged it behind him while crawling through the ditch into his hiding place. It closed the entrance off so well that one needed a pair of sharp eyes to discover the opening. All day long he remained hidden, listening and thinking about his flight to freedom.

Everything in the forest seemed rather quiet but he was so excited that he couldn't sleep. Happily, he hadn't heard any alarming noise, although one time he thought he'd heard some voices from far away. But the faint sounds lasted so briefly and disappeared so soon that he easily could have been mistaken.

The first morning he spent as a hunted animal, nervously listening and watching for any possible alarm, but gradually he had become calmer and his thoughts had turned about the future. Was it good to run away and not to bother about Manette? Deep in his heart he felt that it would be cowardly and mean to desert her while escaping safely himself to Holland. Why couldn't he try to find her in Paris and take her with him, if he wouldn't be caught himself? It couldn't be difficult to find her. Most likely she would be sent to church regularly like all Huguenot children, and it would be rather simple to watch the churchgoers until he saw her. The poor boy didn't have the faintest idea of the large number of churches in Paris. He had heard that it was a large city, which he pictured as two or three villages with an unusually large church. After considering the pros and the cons of this new plan, he decided to go to Paris first to see if he could find Manette.

Having made this decision, he again reviewed his escape plan. He still thought the best plan was his original idea of going west through the forest where nobody would look for him and then turning north. While considering his plans, he suddenly became aware of the possibility that his father might be freed and would look for him and Manette in the village. What a pity that nobody would know where they were!

How could he make sure that his father would find them? It was impossible to send a letter; he didn't even have an address. After spending many hours trying to find a satisfactory solution to this problem, at last he decided to leave a message in the secret cache behind the chimney. Probably, his father would open it and look inside. He could leave a message. Some words scratched in a piece of wood would be enough. While considering this solution, his eyes were already moving around for a suitable piece of wood. He didn't mind not seeing any good material at first glance for he had to return to the cottage again that night to get more water, and it would be easy to break a flat piece of wood from someplace in the house.

In the middle of the night he had taken the risk again to go to the well. Oh, it had been a night that he wouldn't forget easily. At this late hour he had not expected anybody to be looking for him, but still he didn't feel comfortable and several times he nearly had turned back to his hiding place, thinking that he was seeing or hearing frightening things. Once it sounded as if some people were whispering together, and a few moments later he had the impression that somebody was standing under a tree, watching. Of course, it hadn't been true. It was just his imagination.

All the way to the cottage, he was extremely cautious, walking stealthily and even slouching between the bushes. Once, he waited a long time, crouching behind some large trees until he realized that the noise he heard was made by a large deer.

At last he arrived and plunged the pail into the well to get water. The dreadful noise of this simple action had terrified him, for it sounded as if it could be heard for miles and miles. With a small, flat piece of wood broken off from the closet in the cottage, he had hurried back to the hideout. In the meantime, however, the moon had disappeared, and in the pitch dark he had lost his way and couldn't find the field with the thornbushes. After several hours of searching he had given up, and being at his wit's end, had just sat down to wait for the sunrise.

Gradually, the darkness had lessened and at last he had recognized the part of the forest he was in. It was quite a distance away from his hiding place, and it had taken him a long time to go back again. He had been so tired that he had fallen down on his bed of leaves, pine needles, and moss and had been soundly asleep during the rest of the morning until late in the afternoon.

At last he woke up. Yawning, he rubbed his eyes, not awake enough as yet to realize where he was. After a moment he remembered being in the woods, running away from his uncles. Suddenly he stiffened. Loud voices could be heard, which probably had aroused him in the first place. Panic-stricken, he remained in the same position, afraid that he might have been discovered. But nothing happened and his fear lessened somewhat, although the danger still remained very great. In his heart a wordless prayer rose to God to protect and help him.

It seemed that somebody was drinking, for he heard him say, "Well, that tastes good after such a tiring walk."

He recognized the voice instantly. It was the voice of Farmer Lebrun, a neighbor of Uncle Louis. Another voice, the son of Lebrun, whom he also knew well, replied, "It sure does, although I'd rather be drinking a good glass of wine at home than a bucket of water here in the forest. Anybody with brains knows that we are fools to do what Father Francis commands. It's bad enough to chase a boy who has run away, but it's the height of stupidity to do so after he has been gone for two days, especially in this hot weather. I bet that John will be back soon enough when he gets hungry, and if not, so what? I couldn't care less. Anyhow, it isn't worthwhile to do more walking today. I am too tired. I need to take a nap. If Father Francis wants the boy so badly, let him chase him himself. He's a very clever priest who can force me to run another day after the boy!"

An unknown voice said, "It wouldn't be so bad if all the work at home on the farm wasn't waiting, especially now at harvest time when there aren't enough workers available. Just one thunderstorm and all the hay will be so wet that we'll, at the very least, be another week behind with our work."

"Right you are," old Lebrun said. "I wouldn't be surprised if everybody thinks the same as you. I wonder if anybody will come to church tomorrow to continue the search."

"You must be daft to think that nobody will come," grumbled the unknown voice. "There are always a few who expect to merit heaven by obeying Father Francis. But I'm not such a fool. My own work is far more important than the whims of a priest, and if his nephew likes to run away, well, that isn't my business. Anyhow, I am surprised that he could outwit both his uncles. He must have good brains and a good pair of legs, too. He may still be caught, though, for he doesn't know that Father Francis sent letters to all the villages around here."

"Father," asked the young Lebrun, "why do they make such a fuss about him? What difference does it make to Father Francis if he sends John away or he runs away? He's gone and that's what they want, right?"

"I don't know. Father Francis could never get along very well with his brother, John's father. Maybe that has something to do with it."

"Nobody knows," the unknown voice interrupted rudely, "and I don't care to listen to your jabbering. Keep your mouth shut so that I can get some sleep. Maybe I can still do some work tonight if we don't get home too late."

John heard somebody stirring as if he was trying to find a comfortable spot, and after a few minutes it became quiet again. Yet, he remained a long time in the same position until he felt that they must be asleep and only then did he dare to shift his body. He needed to move badly because one of his legs had lain in a cramped position and ached horribly. Because of the tension he was under, he had not given it much attention before, but now the pain became nearly unbearable. Slowly he turned on his back and stretched both his legs out as far as he could. It helped and gradually the cramp disappeared.

He knew that there must be three men close to his hiding place. Very cautiously he lifted his head and looked over the edge of the ditch in the direction of the voices he had heard. Just outside the thornbushes he saw three dark shapes lying on the ground. That must be them, he thought, lying in the shade. It became apparent that all would be lost if they woke up and looked in his direction because the bucket with water was too big to hide completely and was visible through the bushes.

All at once an excellent idea struck him. Very, very slowly he unfolded the blanket he had brought with him, put it over the bucket and covered the bucket with leaves and moss from his improvised bed. Then he laid down comfortably in the ditch again and covered himself over with the remaining leaves and moss. He stretched himself without making any noise, yawned and waited. However, it wasn't as peaceful as he had hoped. To his great chagrin he soon found out that it was so hot underneath his blanket of leaves that he could hardly stand it. He began to perspire and felt as if he would choke but he made up his mind not to give it too much attention for fear that he might betray himself.

In the meantime, he considered all the valuable information he had overheard. It was good to know that they were already tired of running after him. It meant that he could leave at least one day earlier than he had originally planned without increasing the risk of being caught. It would certainly solve his food problem for he was already running very low, not having taken much with him. Besides, not being able to see or to talk to anybody was so hard that he could barely stand it any longer. He felt it would be easier if he could do something, like walking along.

A few hours later somebody moved, yawned noisily and stretched himself.

"Wake up, Lebrun, it's time to go home."

An indistinct muttering was the answer but it must have helped for a few moments later they were ready to leave.

"Well, it was good sleeping here," said young Lebrun looking around. "Strange, I never saw this large field with briars. It looks like a perfect hiding place. Wouldn't it be a good joke if John is hiding in it somewhere?"

John felt himself shake with fright at hearing this. If they suspected he was there, they only needed to wait at the entrance of his secret spot to catch him. Even sneaking away now would not help. Most likely they would see him, and tomorrow the whole village would search the woods thoroughly until he was caught.

"Nonsense," old Lebrun laughed. "Nobody can go through these thornbushes without being torn to pieces. Come on let's go home. It's getting late."

"Wait a moment, Dad. It's not as bad as you think. I've never been scared of a few scratches. I bet that I can go through this field without too much trouble."

"Stop it! We have no time for tomfoolery and your mother has enough to do already without mending your torn clothes."

"Well, why don't you start home now? I'll follow after I've tried my luck with these bushes."

At the same moment, John heard the boy start into the field. John was terrified, for he heard muttered curses and ejaculations of pain but couldn't see anything. After a few moments, which seemed hours to John, the boy yelled, "Dad, you were right. I'm stuck and can't move forward or backward without being scratched by these miserable thorns. Please help me get out of them."

Both men began to laugh and pretended to go away without him but after having enjoyed the fun, they took their knives and cut off the branches that held young Lebrun so tightly that he couldn't back out of the field.

"Have you ever seen such a crazy fool?" old Lebrun scolded. "He always thinks he knows best, and now see what has happened. You will be the laughingstock of the whole village when they see your scratched face. Well, who knows? You may be lucky and have Father Francis believe how hard you worked for him, but I doubt it. Anyway, it would have been smarter to lay on your belly and look along the ground if you really think that John has hidden himself there. At least it would have been much simpler."

Apparently young Lebrun followed his father's advice, for John heard him say, "What is that dark thing underneath the bushes?"

"Oh, I don't know. As far as I'm concerned, it may be the stump of an old tree or an anthill, for that matter! Look, it doesn't move at all. It is certainly not the boy and that is the only thing that counts. He must be far from here, since he has probably used his time better than you."

A few moments later everything had become quiet and calm again. John, feeling happy now that the danger was over, shook off the leaves and other dirt, and crawled along the ditch away from the thornbushes. He stood up, stretched his legs, which had become rather stiff, and walked around a little. It had been a very narrow escape, he thought, but the Lord had protected him. He kneeled down on the sand, giving thanks to his heavenly Father Who had saved him from being caught.

When he opened his eyes, he saw that it had become dark. Ominous black clouds were gathering in the sky. A thunderstorm was coming up after the hot and humid day, and he could see it wouldn't be long before the rain would start. Certainly not an event to look forward to, for he would be drenched in no time and would be feeling very uncomfortable in his wet clothes all night long.

It didn't take him long to make up his mind. It wouldn't be likely for them to search at night during a thunderstorm. Sleeping in the cottage tonight wouldn't be too risky, he decided. He rushed back into the hiding place, emptied the water bucket, threw his food into it, grasped his blanket, and dashed to the cottage. Just as the first drops of rain began to fall he reached the cottage.

After folding his blanket, he placed it on the floor and seated himself comfortably on it. He leaned against the wall of the room while he was wide awake, since he had slept most of the day. He decided to wait one more day, and then leave. The first few days he needed to be very careful but if he traveled at night and hid in the daytime, things would work out. It would take about twelve hours to go through the forest, which he could do easily in two or three nights. Having lived all his life in the woods, he wasn't overly concerned about the wild animals. Wolves were cowards in summertime and would never dare to attack, and he hoped to avoid any wild swine that might come his direction. It was a pity that he only had his knife to defend himself but a strong club was also a good weapon. Then he remembered his axe. Anyhow, the most dangerous part of his journey would be over when he had gone through the forest.

The thunderstorm ended at midnight and the next morning the sun rose again in a cloudless sky. At daybreak, John carved the words 'I have left for Holland, John' into a piece of wood, and put it in the secret enclosure after taking the money and the necklace. He searched the cottage for the last time but didn't find anything, so he left.

Back in the hiding place he spread his blanket on the ground and quickly fell soundly asleep. When he awoke he remembered only that the wet ground had soaked his blanket, giving him an unpleasant feeling, even in his sleep.

7

MOTHER ROSETTE'S HELP

Three days later, John had put quite a distance between himself and his native village. Every night he had walked for hours and hours without resting much. The first night, after his forced rest in the hiding place, he had managed to cover a large distance by following trails that were somewhat familiar. The first morning he hadn't even looked for a sleeping place but continued walking because he wanted to leave the dangerous area, where somebody might outpace him, as soon as possible. After this successful start, walking had become more difficult, for it was so dark the next night that he had lost the trail, and was forced to find his way around all different kinds of bushes. In the early morning of the second day he was far from sure of the proper direction but felt rather confident that he was at least going away from the village, and the rest didn't matter too much. During the daytime he had slept, hidden underneath some bushes where he felt safe. Both evenings he had resumed his walk as soon as the sun began to set, but the going had been difficult in the dark until the moon appeared late at night.

The country he passed through changed gradually. The first night he had seen mainly trees interspersed with shrubs and wild bramble bushes. After that he had seen small, grassy, open clearings with groups of trees. Early in the morning the open areas became larger and larger, although he still saw many trees. Once in a while he passed a farm surrounded by cultivated fields, and a few times he saw a single cow or some sheep.

That night his troubles began. He must have stepped on something sharp because one spot underneath his left foot became rather sore. At first, he didn't pay much attention to it, but when the pain became worse and worse, he examined the sore spot as well as he could in the dark without discovering anything wrong. By walking on the toe of that foot he could maintain his regular pace for a short time, but later the pain increased and he was forced to slow down. The worst was yet to come for he got a large blister on the heel of his other foot, and he could barely limp along. Even so he clenched his teeth and kept going until the early morning. A field with ripe wheat provided an easy hiding place where he could rest. Sleeping was impossible no matter how hard he tried because he was too tired and hungry, and the hot sun didn't improve things, either. Happily the pain in his feet lessened after resting the whole day but in the evening when he continued his walk again it increased gradually. Yet, he didn't dare to take a longer rest for he had run out of food two days earlier and hadn't eaten since. He was beginning to feel miserable and weak with hunger.

Fortunately, the forest and its wearisome going was definitely behind him. Now he could walk along a small trail, and he sometimes saw tiny houses or small farms. Every time he passed one he thought about knocking on the door but never did because he was afraid of awakening the people in the middle of the night. However, he knew that he couldn't go on like this much longer. His limping had already changed to a kind of stumbling along, and he was so tired and pained that he nearly collapsed. Just in time he found an old, deserted barn in a field where he could lay on some old straw. He was dizzy and felt as if everything around him turned one way or another. It was impossible to sleep, for all kinds of feverish ideas raced through his mind. At last, late in the morning he fell into a troublesome slumber from which he awoke at the end of the afternoon. Faint with hunger and barely able to stand on his sore feet he doggedly went on his way again, tottering along like a drunk.

Slowly, wearily he crossed the field until he found a small dirt road going in the proper direction. He took it because the path was somewhat easier. After awhile he arrived at a small, wooden cottage with a shabby, weather-beaten appearance. In front of the house were three old, gnarled, fruit trees and next to it was a partially filled haystack. Nobody seemed to be around, not even a cat or dog. Everything was quiet.

Who knows? he thought. The house might be empty so that I can stay overnight.

He barely had the courage to ask help from strangers. When they asked questions that he couldn't afford to answer for safety's sake they might bring him to the priest and then everything would be lost. Yet, staying in this house a few nights wouldn't solve his food problem. Not knowing exactly what to do, he seated himself on the grass in front of the house, and waited to see if anybody would appear, but no one did.

After what felt like a long time, he became impatient and went to the front door, which was locked from the inside. He saw at once how easily it could be opened, for running through the door were large cracks that he could put his hand through and lift the bolt on the inside. Nevertheless, he hesitated, wondering if it wouldn't be better to explore the back of the house first. Maybe it had a useful rear door so that no casual passer-by would see him enter the house.

He hobbled around the corner of the cottage, but suddenly stood still as if deadlocked. Seeing an old woman, sitting on her knees in a kind of kitchen-garden, came as a real shock to him after having convinced himself that the house must be deserted. Evidently, she had been so busy with her work that she hadn't heard him at all.

Presently she looked up and saw John, who didn't know what to say. Her unfriendly face made him feel uneasy and shy. He decided that the woman must be old for she had gray hair, and her face was full of wrinkles. What scared him most were her eyes, jet-black and piercing, as if she could look straight through him.

"What are you doing here?" she asked sulkily.

"Nothing," John replied, so frightened that he completely forgot his hunger and painful feet. He wondered if it wouldn't be better to run away from her, but he felt that she could easily catch up with him because she looked rather healthy and determined.

"Nothing?" she repeated slowly. "Come on, don't be afraid. Who sent you? Is someone sick at home? Did your mother send you to buy herbs? What is it?"

"I have no mother," he stated unnecessarily.

"Oh, I see, just wandering around, are you? Begging, stealing, and doing mischief, and of course, too lazy to work."

"I'm not too lazy to work and I'm hungry."

"That is fine. Let's make a bargain. You help me with the weeding and afterwards I'll give you something to eat."

Hesitantly he stepped carefully on his sore feet into the garden to find out what she wanted him to do. She watched him closely and suddenly said, "Wait a moment, what is the matter with you? You walk as if you are in pain. Is something wrong with your feet?" She stood up, came to him, and suddenly saw how tired and hungry he looked.

"When was the last time you ate?" she asked abruptly.

"Oh, a few days ago," he said softly with his eyes cast down.

"Come into the house," she ordered him. "I thought that you were fooling me but I am not such a brute as to put you to work when you are hungry and have pain." And without looking at him anymore she went into the house through the rear door.

Inside the house it was deliciously cool. It consisted of only one room which, apparently, was also used as a stable, for in one of the corners was a pile of hay for a goat. The floor was made of clay and not very clean. Two wooden chairs and a rickety table was all the furniture John saw. On a few shelves, attached to the wall, was an assortment of pots and pans and other gadgets. He also saw a pile of old rags, which seemed to be used as a bed. Everything looked filthy and it smelled strong.

"Sit down," she said as she went to the shelves where she fetched a piece of bread. "I haven't wine or beer but you can have some goat's milk if you like."

In a twinkling John ate a very substantial meal of bread, cheese, and milk. He felt much better afterwards and nervously expected that the woman would ask all kind of questions that he couldn't answer without giving himself away. Nothing like that happened for she waited until he was ready and then said, "Let me examine your feet now." She knelt on the floor in front of him and scrutinized his feet thoroughly.

"Mmm, a couple of blisters and a nice infection. Did you step on a thorn?"

John shrugged his shoulders without saying anything.

"Well, you are fortunate that you came here for I know how to treat such things. Just stay where you are until I have dressed your feet."

She went over to the fireplace to prepare a dressing for his feet. Some pieces of wood were still glowing underneath a layer of ash. She threw some more wood on top, and with the help of a pair of old bellows, quickly had a roaring fire. Next, she filled a large cauldron with water and hung it over the fire. After examining his feet again, she returned to the fireplace and picked a few herbs, which were hanging down from a nail in the ceiling and threw them into the boiling water. She let the water boil a while, and then removed the pot from the fire, and placed it on the floor to cool down. As soon as the mixture had reached the proper temperature, she took some rags, dipped them into the pot, and wrapped them around John's feet.

"That will do," she said pleasantly. "A few days rest until the infection breaks open and then you will again be as good as new."

She picked up the other chair, moved it opposite John, and seated herself. All the preparations for his feet had taken such a long time that it had become nearly dark in the room except for the light from the fireplace.

"Time to go to bed," she said, "But before we go to sleep I would like to know more about you." John moved uneasily on his chair, and made up his mind as he had done before, to say as little as possible, although he felt it wouldn't be easy to hide anything from this shrewd woman. She was watching him attentively, which made him nervous.

"Why didn't you stay with your father when your mother died?" she asked him after awhile.

"I haven't seen my father for many years. I don't know where he might be," John replied hesitantly.

"Oh, I see! But where are you going now? Don't you have relatives, uncles or aunts? Was there nobody in the village who was willing to take care of you? Which village do you come from?"

John didn't know how to evade her penetrating questions, but he did his best to give satisfactory answers without telling too much.

"I lived with my mother, until she passed away, in a cottage in the forest where my father was a game warden. I've only a little sister left, in Paris. Her name is Manette and I am on my way to see her."

"You want to go to Paris?" the woman exclaimed, astonished. "How do you expect to get there? It will mean many weeks of walking. Where will you sleep at night, and how will you get food? You will never get there!"

"I can sleep outside," John said patiently, "as I have done the last few nights. I am not lazy and am certainly willing to work for my food."

She didn't ask anything else, but watched him reflectively. At last she remarked, "Either you don't know how far it is to Paris or something else is the matter. Anyhow, what is your name?"

"My name is John!"

"Good. Everybody calls me Mother Rosette and you can do the same. Let's go to bed now. You must sleep in the straw with the goat. I'll get her from outside."

She went outside and returned a few moments later with a big goat, which she tied up in a corner atop the straw. John followed her, and lay down on the straw. He heard the old woman shuffle to the pile of rags and go to bed there.

Before John went to sleep he folded his hands to say his evening prayer. He was very thankful that he had come to this house and that Mother Rosette had helped him. Afterward he stayed awake a short time wondering if she had understood why he was roaming around. He was so tired that he fell asleep before he had found an answer to his question.

8

A SCARY EXPERIENCE IN A CARRIAGE

John stayed with Mother Rosette for five days and enjoyed every one of them. Fortunately, the infection in his foot wasn't as bad as she initially thought, and her medication had done miracles. It was nearly healed and bothered him very little. His walking was nearly as good as before his flight. Most of the time, especially the last few days, he had given Mother Rosette a helping hand with her garden and not a single weed was left. It was a rather strange kitchen garden with very few vegetables and lots of special herbs, most of them not known to John. Mother Rosette had explained that she grew and gathered herbs for a physician in the city. Every morning she rose early and picked them when they were still wet from the dew, for that is when they had the best healing effect. Then she strung the herbs onto thin ropes and dried them in the sun.

John soon found out that most people were afraid of Mother Rosette. Nobody ever came to see her except when they were sick and needed her herbs. Most people failed to show their gratitude, gossiping in the village that she was a witch, who had the power to make a person healthy or sick by just looking at him in a particular way. To John, however, she had been friendly, and he liked her a lot. They didn't talk to each other much, only a few words after supper when it was too dark to work, but it was enough for John to realize how lonely she was.

Today, feeling healthy and rested again, he made up his mind that he should leave for Holland the following morning. Telling Mother Rosette would be unpleasant for he knew that she liked his company rather well. However, the conversation turned out much easier than he had expected.

After supper, before John could say anything, she put her chair outside the door of the cottage, and told him to do the same.

"I need to talk to you tonight, John," she said in a friendly voice. "The last few days I've thought about it a lot and now, at last, I've decided what to do. I want you to do me a real favor but first I must tell you more about myself so that you'll understand why."

She waited a few moments, apparently considering how to begin, and then continued.

"I haven't always lived alone in this cottage. Long ago I had a fine family with my husband and my son Jacob. He looked after the land, and I took care of Jacob. We had to work hard but enjoyed it and were happy. When my son was five years old, my husband passed away. I became poor, but managed to bring my son up decently, and he became a fine boy. When Jacob was about seventeen, he told me that he didn't want to live in this desolate part of the country anymore and went to Marseille to become a sailor. A boy raised on a farm never becomes a good sailor, and after a few years he came back. He couldn't get used to living here after having been away so long, though, and went to Paris looking for work. He did rather well and nowadays owns a small inn, called *In The Fishing Cat*. Every year he sends a letter and some money. The priest always reads me the letter, since I can't read and then I tell the priest what to write to Jacob, which he is always more than willing to do.

"Anyway, I've been alone for many years and that's not right. I'm getting old and need some help. It is getting too hard for me to gather herbs. Would you like to stay with me? I would love to have you around. It struck me the last few days that you seem to dislike talking about yourself and your family. If you are running away or trying to hide from something, mind, you don't need to tell me anything. I think that I can guess why you want to go to Paris, though! I wouldn't be surprised to hear that you are a Huguenot because I have never seen you cross yourself, not even before meals like every good Roman Catholic does. You are certainly not a beggar and it is strange, to say the least, that you don't know where your father is. Most likely he is in jail. You haven't mentioned any other relatives, either. Orphan boys like you are taken care of by their relatives or by the church. They aren't allowed to wander around on their own. I think that your story about going to Paris to live with your sister is nothing but a part of your imagination. Maybe you plan to go to Paris because it's harder to be caught in a big city.

"Now listen, don't tell me if my guesses are right or wrong. As long as I don't know for sure everything is fine, but I risk the harsh punishment of the priest for helping you if I know for sure that you are a Huguenot. Anyway, you are relatively safe here in my cottage.

Nobody will see you since I live a fair distance from the village and rarely have visitors, as you must have noticed. Why not stay with me? Isn't that far better than wandering along the roads or going to Paris?"

She stopped talking, and he felt her looking at him. He wondered how to explain that he couldn't take her friendly but unexpected offer. It was crucial not to mention that he was a Huguenot, but what good reason could he give her for not staying? She must know that he would love to stay with her!

"Mother Rosette," he said slowly, "I can't stay although I would like to. It's true that I have a little sister in Paris and that I am on my way to see her. She is younger than I and her name is Manette. I haven't told you much about her for I thought it better not to tell you all my plans. Even now I'm afraid to say too much, but if you knew everything, you would understand that I really can't stay with you although it's hard for me to go. If my sister Manette . . ." Here the boy stopped short, suddenly wondering if he had already said too much. Mother Rosette, hearing how nervous John was, didn't answer at once, giving him some time to calm down. After a while she tried again to get his promise to stay, but to no avail. John had made up his mind that he would try to save Manette and take her to Holland.

At last Mother Rosette said disappointed, "I see that I can't persuade you to stay with me and, maybe you're right. It is such a pity because I felt especially the last days as if my own Jacob had returned. Well, it can't be helped! When do you intend to leave?"

"I figured I would leave tomorrow morning," John answered hesitantly. A few moments elapsed while she quietly considered how to help John further.

"It's better to wait a few more days. I may be able to help you a little if somebody in the village is going in the same direction as you. True, the people in the village dislike me but they are enough afraid of me to do what I ask. Better wait until I know more. By the way, do you have any money? Not that I want it, but I can advise you how to use it properly."

Confidently, John showed her the golden coin which he kept in his pocket. Mother Rosette was extremely surprised to find him with such a large treasure.

"Where did you get that from? I haven't seen so much money for many a long year."

"My mother left it for me," John replied proudly, "but I want to give it to you. I don't know what would have happened if you hadn't helped me."

Mother Rosette laughed. "What a big child you are. You haven't any idea how much this gold is worth! If you could have it exchanged, it would bring you quite a way to Paris, but right now it's useless for nobody will give you change without suspecting that you have stolen it. You know what I'll do? I'll sew it into your trouser band so that you cannot show or lose it."

"But Mother Rosette, I may have to use it if I become sick again and have to sleep at an inn."

"No, John, it can't be done. As I said, you would be treated as a thief. Besides, you can't even sleep in an inn without paying taxes. Everybody must do that, and the innkeeper must charge the taxes to his guests if they haven't paid them to the taxcollectors. If he knew that you have so much money, he would never give you your change back and would pocket it himself. While talking about innkeepers, you know what you should do? Go to my son in Paris who owns *In The Fishing Cat*. When you tell him that you have been here, he will certainly help you and give you the proper change. Tomorrow I will sew the coin in your trouser band. That is much safer while traveling."

A few days later, a large coach left the village, and John was sitting with the coachman on the front seat. It was the traveling coach of the Marquis who owned many villages and estates in that area and lived with his family in a castle close to the village. John felt as if he were dreaming, sitting on the coachman's seat just behind the horses. Mind, he had never in his life seen such a large carriage and only a few times ridden on an old farmer's cart. Imagine, today he was sitting on the front seat of the traveling coach of a real marquis. He thought it nothing less than a miracle what Mother Rosette had been able to accomplish, for the Marquis was never concerned about or interested in common people.

Yet, it hadn't been difficult at all for Mother Rosette to arrange. She had heard that a servant was going to drive the empty coach to Clermont, pick up the wife and daughter of the Marquis who were staying with some relatives, and bring them back to their castle. Immediately she went to the steward who supervised all the servants of the Marquis and told him that she had cured a sick boy who needed to go with the traveling coach. At first the man objected vehemently, but when she hinted darkly about all kinds of diseases that might hit him and his family, he gave in. The reason was simple. He was a superstitious man. He pictured himself and his whole family deathly sick in bed due to Mother Rosette's sinister powers. Therefore the steward meekly gave permission for John to travel with the coach on the condition it picked him up outside the village so that nobody would see it. Obviously, Mother Rosette agreed with his stipulation. Before dawn the next morning the coachman had stopped and told John to take a seat next to him.

The coachman was a rough, young fellow who was told by the steward to leave the boy alone and not to ask any questions. The steward stressed the severe punishment that he would receive if he mentioned to anybody that he was taking the boy with him. It all sounded rather mysterious to the coachman, and he wondered why he must handle this boy with kids gloves. The first few hours he kept quiet and watched John furtively. John wasn't inclined to talk, either, for he was still upset about saying goodbye to Mother Rosette. He had begun to love her and felt very sorry for them both that he had to leave. As a matter of fact, Mother Rosette had barely been able to hold her tears back, either. Gradually, however, when the sun began to rise, he became so interested in the scenery and the traffic on the road that at last he didn't think about her anymore.

In the meantime his companion, the coachman, hadn't seen anything outstanding in the boy. He seemed to be a very common boy. Maybe his boss had exaggerated his importance. He decided that talking wouldn't do any harm and might give a clue about why this boy was getting such special treatment. Curious to know who John really was, he began by asking John his name. John told him. After some further prodding and questioning by the coachman, John began chatting happily, forgetting to be cautious about his remarks, although he avoided mentioning he was a Huguenot heading for his little sister in Paris. Listening quietly, the coachman became more and more convinced that there was something unusual about John, and he began contemplating what it was. Looking at his honest face, he didn't think that he was a criminal or common beggar. After all the very fact that the steward had given him permission to go with the coach indicated that it must be something else. After pondering a long while, he wondered if he could be a Huguenot fleeing the country, but the following moment he doubted his own suspicion. Many Huguenots were indeed fleeing, but it seemed to him that John was rather young for such a thing. Besides, if it were true, John would be traveling toward the southern border and not to the north as they were heading now. However, it was even less likely that the boy was a criminal. And so he kept wondering about John while continuing the conversation by telling about the cities he had visited with his master.

While they were chatting together, the coachman thought out a devilish plan. He believed without a doubt that something was wrong with the boy and felt that it was a good bet that the boy was a heretic. He decided that it wouldn't be a bad idea to deliver him into the hands of a priest or judge. If his guess was right, he would definitely pocket some money! If it was wrong . . . so what? It wasn't likely that the steward would ever find out, and if he did, would he be willing to admit that he had allowed this boy a free ride?

John enjoyed the trip immensely. They drove all day, stopping a few times at nice cool places along the road to rest the horse. In the afternoon, after having passed through several small villages, he saw a large group of various church steeples fairly close by. It must be a city, John thought, and was correct, for his companion explained that he couldn't take John any further because he had to pick up the family of the Marquis and return tomorrow. The horse, which was hitched to the coach, would be left behind and two fresh horses would be supplied for tomorrow's ride, so the return trip would take less time.

"It is, of course, rather foolish for you to ride with me into the city where everybody can see you sitting on this bench. Maybe the best thing is for you to go your own way as soon as we are close to the city limits. Don't you agree? Anyway I have to stop and deliver a message to an innkeeper. Wait . . . now that I think about it, you can do me a favor by watching the horse while I step inside the inn for a few moments. I don't like to leave the horse alone and it'll take only a few minutes. You don't mind, do you?"

Obviously, John didn't mind at all giving this friendly man a helping hand. He knew little about inns and was unaware that innkeepers, and not travelers, took care of the horses and carriages. Presently they arrived at the inn and jumped off the coach, glad that this part of the journey was over. The coachman flung the reins to John, and disappeared without much ado, after repeating that he would be back shortly.

John caught the reins and held them loosely in his hands, but soon realized that it was absurd. In front of the inn was a row of stakes where travelers tied their horses. Why should he then hold onto the horse himself? It would be more pleasant if he didn't have to remain standing in one spot and could walk around. Carefully he guided the horse to one of the stakes, threw the reins over it to secure the animal, and began to walk up and down.

After waiting some time for the coachman to return, he stopped walking and stood next to the horse, petting her proud neck absent-mindedly. After a while it struck him how beautiful the carriage was. It was an impressive sight to see such a well-maintained coach with the coat-of-arms of the Marquis painted on the doors. Having admired the outside of the coach, he became curious how such a magnificent carriage looked inside. He went to one of the windows and tried to peer through while standing on his toes but didn't see much because the glass was caked with dirt from the roads. He made a little spyhole by rubbing the dirt off with a wet finger, but that revealed little, for it was too dark inside the carriage. Why shouldn't he open the door? he thought. The coachman was a friendly fellow who would understand how curious he was to see the inside of such a beautiful carriage.

Very carefully, he opened the door and saw that it had two seats opposite each other that were covered with a kind of tapestry. In his whole life he had never seen such a rich covering. Gingerly, he touched it, caressing the cloth with his hand. How good it felt! he knew it must be extremely expensive, though. To be a marquis, to sit in this couch and be driven to any place you like, must be wonderful, he thought. What fun it would be to sit on this beautiful seat, just like a son of the marquis.

He looked around, and seeing that the street was empty, slipped inside, and closed the door.

It certainly felt nice and comfortable, but he wasn't at ease and after a few minutes of quiet enjoyment wanted to get out of the carriage. But at the very moment that he grasped the knob to open the door, he saw the coachman coming, accompanied by two soldiers.

"What shall I do now?" he asked himself. They would see him leaving the coach if he opened the door. Suddenly he wasn't sure anymore that the coachman wouldn't be angry. Besides, why did he bring these soldiers? Did they plan to put him in jail? He decided the safest thing to do was to lie down on the floor between the two benches and remain as quiet as possible.

The men came closer and he heard the surprised exclamation of the coachman when he didn't see John.

"Where can that boy be? I left him to watch the horse and I am sure that he didn't suspect anything. He couldn't have run away. We would have seen him coming down the street. Let's ask the innkeeper. He may have seen him or might know where he has gone."

John's heart sank into his boots when he realized that he was trapped. He had absolutely forgotten that they were standing in front of the inn. They could have watched him all the time through the windows and would surely not have any trouble catching him. He also understood that the coachman intended to deliver him into the hands of the soldiers, but he didn't have the faintest idea why. The fellow couldn't possibly have figured out that he was a Huguenot, he reflected. Or could he have guessed it, like Mother Rosette? Presently, the men returned with the innkeeper.

"No, I don't waste my time by looking through windows. Why would I? There aren't many people on the street at this time of the day, anyway, and I'm needed inside when travelers stop at my inn. Well, he hasn't been inside the inn, either, for I would have seen him. Why do you want him so much?"

"Well," answered the coachman, "I thought that this boy was a Huguenot and such people are better in jail or on the galleys."

"Come on, fellow," one of the soldiers grumbled, "Where is the boy? Find him or make up for it! You came tearing into the guardhouse and promised half of the money you would get if we brought the boy to the priest. I'm not overly interested in that boy, but very much interested in the money. We didn't come with you to be fooled by your stupidity!"

"Yes," the other soldier backed him, "give the boy or the money. It is easy to make promises but now you had better keep them!"

"But I haven't any money. I'm just a poor coachman. After all, it's your own fault that the boy has escaped. If you hadn't wasted so much time, the boy would still be here."

Both soldiers became furious when they heard that he had no money to pay them.

"You'd better pay," one soldier said, threateningly. "If you don't spit up the money, it will be worse for you."

The other soldier grasped the coachman by his collar and said, "You just come with us to the guardhouse, and then we'll hear what the captain thinks about your tomfoolery. A night in jail will make you more pliable, I think. Come on, Balthasar, give me a hand and we'll take him with us."

The soldier didn't have much success, though, for the coachman tore himself loose and hit him so hard that he flew against the fence that was attached to the side of the inn. Nevertheless, it would have gone badly for the coachman if the innkeeper, not wanting a brawl in front of his place, hadn't interfered. He had to remain good friends with the soldiers who came frequently to his inn for drinks, and at the same time had to make sure not to run into trouble with the Marquis if his coachman was maltreated.

"No, gentlemen," he called. "Stop fighting! I know a better solution. The coachman claims that he is as poor as a church mouse, but he can always afford the cost of a few drinks. I'm sure that you can't get more out of him even if you turn him upside down and shake him loose. Come in, have a few drinks and let him pay for it."

After another few angry words and remarks, all three agreed and grudgingly, the coachman went inside with them. A few seconds later, a boy came out of the inn and watched the street. The innkeeper, who also liked to earn some extra money, was smart enough to have the street watched in case the runaway would turn up. No doubt, it was a waste of the boy's time for John, terrified, didn't dare to stir. He felt as if any moment someone might realize the obvious and open the door to inspect the inside of the coach. He was trapped and had no chance whatsoever to escape and therefore he stayed where he was.

Apparently, the coachman didn't like it very much in the inn for he returned in a remarkably short time, jumped onto his seat and drove away like a madman. John, happy that they were riding again, calmed down for he knew that the immediate danger of being discovered was over. He wasn't safe, though, for he had to get out of the coach without being discovered. He couldn't leap out of it without the people in the street seeing it and he knew no other way.

Cautiously peeping through one of the windows, he saw that they were no longer riding on a country road but through the streets of a city. Before he knew what to do, the carriage suddenly turned around a corner and drove through a wide gate. It stopped in the inner court of a large building. He had barely time to duck when he heard loud voices and footsteps. They had arrived at their destination and there he was, trapped in a coach, surrounded by servants!

Fortunately, nobody thought to open the carriage door. The horse was unharnessed, and several men pushed the coach into the coach house. The last thing he heard was somebody giving orders that the coach must be cleaned before the next morning. The doors of the coach house closed, and he was alone again.

9

WINDOWS ARE CONVENIENT

John felt much relieved that he wasn't discovered. To get out of the coach, however, was clearly the first thing to do before somebody came in and began cleaning the carriage. He glanced through the window to make sure that nobody was around, opened the coach door and jumped lightly to the floor. He was in a large, spacious room with two more carriages and still enough open space to walk comfortably around, any one of them.

The rear wall had two small windows, and there were two large entrance doors for the carriages in the front. In one of the corners was a ladder leading to the attic. Before he began to look around in the building, he tiptoed to its entrance, hoping to find a small gap through which he could see the court. Perhaps he could disappear through the gate if it was deserted.

Fortunately he hadn't made any noise for when he came close to the entrance he heard voices outside. Through a knothole in the door he saw several men and boys sitting against the doors in front of the coach house. They were rather quiet. Once in a while someone made a remark about the weather or such, but then they remained silent again for a long time. John listened for several minutes. He expected them to gossip about his disappearance at the inn, but it wasn't mentioned at all.

At last one of them stood up, stretched himself slowly and said, "Well, I'd better begin cleaning up the coach before it gets too dark to do a good job." Nobody paid him any attention.

"Move over a bit," he said to the men sitting with their backs against the door, "so I can go inside." Slowly they moved aside and the door opened wide. John, of course, had not waited for him to enter. He had silently gone to the second floor, hoping to find a place where he could hide. This floor had a low ceiling and was divided into several small rooms. Apparently, it was a kind of storeroom for tools and supplies. Scattered everywhere were horse harnesses, pieces of old leather straps, bridles, covers, parts of carriages and even a few carriage wheels. A thick layer of dust covered everything, including the ground, showing that people rarely paid a visit to this floor. Several large closets were built along one of the walls. He opened the door to one of them and found that he could just stand inside without hitting his head. It was very uncomfortable, though, because the closet was dirty and dusty and scorchingly hot.

Downstairs, several men were now busy cleaning the coach and making a great deal of noise. It all sounded so close by that he would like to have shut the closet door tight but didn't dare for fear of suffocating. However, any person who climbed the ladder could be heard soon enough, so he thought he would have ample time to close the door promptly, if necessary.

Fortunately, the cleaning did not take long. They left the coach house late in the afternoon, sometime before sunset. When they were gone, John went to the rear of the attic where he looked through the two little windows, similar to the ones on the first floor. He discovered that he could see a large part of the street, which was separated from the inner court by a wall. The coach house was attached at either side to larger buildings which extended as far as the outer wall so that a small, closed-off yard was formed. This was an important discovery, even more so because the buildings had no windows facing the yard. It would be a perfectly safe place for him.

The outer wall wasn't very high, no more than eight or nine feet. He studied it carefully while trying not to show himself to the people on the street. It was, of course, too high to climb without a ladder, which he didn't have. Still, he felt confident that he could improvise something to use as a ladder by using some of the rubble in the coach house.

After a while, he went downstairs to examine the first floor windows in the rear of the building, which were the only means of entering the yard. Both were closed with a simple latch, which could be easily removed. He opened one of them and saw that the wall was close, no more than seven feet away. The window frame was wide enough to let him pass through, but it would be difficult to return to the coach house when he was outside. Therefore, he had to throw everything he needed for scaling the wall into the yard before he climbed through the window. A thorough search of the coach house was disappointing. He didn't find anything useful except two sturdy beams, four feet long, which he thought might serve his purpose.

He knew it would be foolish to climb the wall during daylight hours. Passersby might think that he was a burglar. He had to wait until after dark. In the meantime, though, he could make the necessary preparations. Carefully, without making much noise, he opened one of the windows and dropped the beams through it into the yard. Next, he grasped the window sill with both his hands and pulled himself so high that he could sit on it with his legs outside the window. The rest was rather simple. He turned on his belly and let himself glide down. With a small jump he fell to the ground. That was done! Fortunately, nobody seemed to have seen him for he heard nothing suspicious, and patiently he sat down on the ground, waiting for darkness.

Waiting always seems long, but John felt as if the hours crept along slower than a snail's pace. At last it was dark enough to try the more risky part of his escape. He put the two beams close together against the wall. Then he placed one of his knees on them and began to pull his other leg up. However, he wasn't even halfway through when the beams began to slide and he fell to the ground.

He did not hurt himself much, but it scared him to think that he could break his neck if he wasn't careful. He tried again, this time by making the beams touch at the top while the other ends were standing far apart on the ground. In this way, the tops of the beams were now lower than before but the whole contraption was far more stable and couldn't slide away easily. He placed one of his knees on top of his "ladder" and very, very slowly pulled up his other knee. Although the whole thing was shaking frightfully, he managed to keep his balance. When he tried to stand up and grasp the edge of the wall, though, it collapsed, and he tumbled to the ground again. This time he wasn't so fortunate for his head hit the brick wall with a resounding whack. He saw all black before his eyes and then felt dizzy before he could see again. It took a long time before he felt well enough to make another attempt. Two additional tries also failed, but at last he managed to get hold of the edge of the wall. He pulled himself up and a moment later was at its top, suddenly feeling tired. He tried in vain to detect if anyone was passing by in the street, but the darkness prevented him from seeing anything. Well, if he couldn't see anything, they wouldn't be able to see him either, he thought, and took the risk of blindly leaping down. Fortunately, the wall wasn't high. He landed safely on the ground in the street without anybody noticing.

The climbing attempts had taken lots of time and it was now close to midnight. Suddenly he realized that the city gates were closed at night, so it was impossible to leave the city. To make things worse, he couldn't remain on the streets, either, for he would be in a dangerous and awkward position if the patrolling night watch found him. They would interrogate him and probably lock him up, for a boy of his age was not allowed to roam along the streets at this time of night. What could he do? he wondered. Where could he, a village boy, go in an unknown city? Good advice would certainly be welcome. He must find a place where he could hide until the morning, but that was nearly impossible. It was so dark he could see nothing but the stars in the sky.

Hesitantly, he began to walk to at least lengthen the distance between himself and the house where he had spent such disagreeable hours. Slowly feeling his way along the street, he tried to figure out what to do next. It was impossible to go to an inn, for even if he could find one in the dark he couldn't explain how he had entered after the city gates were closed. Besides, he remembered clearly the warning from Mother Rosette not to sleep in an inn because of the taxes. Yet, it was most important to get off the streets. He racked his brains to find a solution and, at last, had a wonderful idea. He remembered having seen a church up the street when he had looked through the windows of the coach house. Churches were always open, day and night. He could sneak into that church and hide in a dark corner until the sun rose. Then he could walk out quietly just as if he had attended the first Mass. In a better mood and more cheerful, he began to walk with a purpose and soon arrived at the church building. As he had anticipated, the doors were wide open.

He entered and found that the church was dimly lit by a few candles on the altar and in front of a few images of saints. Nobody was in the church except a few stray dogs, curled up and asleep near the entrance. The best place to stay was, he decided, as close as possible to the doors so that he could sneak out before the first Mass was served. Obviously, it was impossible to find a hiding place in the near darkness, but why should he look for it? When people entered the church, he could walk around a bit and pretend to be a visitor himself. Reassured by his own thoughts, he seated himself comfortably on the floor with his back against the door post of a cupboard. This, he felt, was certainly near enough to the church doors. His single hope was that he wouldn't fall asleep while waiting for the morning.

It was a very strange feeling to be in a Roman Catholic church. In his worst dreams he had never expected to enter it again voluntarily. He remembered everything his mother had told him about the wrong things of the Roman church and about the wicked life of many of the priests. He wondered why so many people remained faithful to this church and didn't want to hear about its heresies. The church was beautifully decorated. Most of the ornaments were given to thank the saints for answering prayers and helping people. John knew better. Saints couldn't hear or answer prayers or help. Only Jesus Christ could help His people and save them from all their sins and misery.

In the darkness of the church he folded his hands and prayed to his heavenly Father. He didn't only ask for forgiveness of his sins, but told Him also how thankful he was that his mother had taught him to go directly to Him in the name of the Lord Jesus Christ and not to trust in saints and other idolatries.

10

JOHN FINDS A FRIEND

It was five o'clock in the morning when Madame Noirette, the wife of the sexton of St. Paul's Church, woke up. She never needed warning that it was time to rise and she was proud of it. As long as she had been married — and that was a long time, forty-three years to be exact — she began the day with the same routine. First, she sat up in bed and yawned, then she rubbed her eyes and yawned again. Next she picked up her rosary which she kept underneath her pillow and prayed. Next, she stepped out of bed. It had to be done rather carefully by first putting her right foot on the floor. She was extremely superstitious and was always afraid that something might go wrong if she started the day by using her left foot first. Then she put her feet in the slippers standing beside the bed and walked to the little cracked mirror on the wall where she pulled a dirty comb through her hair. She never washed herself early in the morning and quite often forgot it during the rest of the day!

Next as a dutiful housewife, she prepared a light breakfast, very light indeed, consisting of a boiled egg and a glass of good wine. After that the most difficult job of the whole day, awaking her husband! It had to be done very carefully because he would be in an ugly mood if he woke up too suddenly. Therefore, she always pretended not to do it on purpose. She would start by talking to herself and would say something like, "Well, let's first boil the eggs before waking up the old man." Obviously, it wouldn't help much, but that didn't bother her. Then she would make more noise by putting her shoes on and purposely stepping loudly around the room. Often, that was enough for her husband to realize sleepily that a new day had started, but the real awakening came when she brought his breakfast and pushed him softly against the shoulder. Today, all her efforts were in vain.

He didn't stir, not even after she put his breakfast next to him on the bed. Surprised and even slightly worried, she lost no time and pushed him much harder than usual. The sexton let out a heavy sigh and grumbled, "Can't you make less noise while preparing breakfast? It's no use pushing me over, either. Stop it and leave me alone. Go away! I am sick. I can't go to church today. You must go without me!"

"Sick? What is the matter?" she asked, amazed.

"I don't know. I feel sore all over and have a terrible headache, my neck is stiff, and I am sick to my stomach. I didn't sleep the whole night, but you don't care! You . . . you kept sleeping the whole time."

His wife said nothing. She had been awake more than once, but every time he had been asleep. However, she knew better than to tell him that.

"Do you want anything else to eat or to drink?" she asked kindly.

"Yes, I'm waiting for my glass of wine. You should have given me that an hour ago!"

He turned around and sat up in his bed with a scowl on his face. Yes, he must be sick, his wife decided. He surely looked it. His eyes were swollen and she saw that he had trouble moving his head. He must have caught a cold! A few days in bed would be good for him.

The wine seemed to revive his spirits a little because he said, "Today you must go to church alone. Put new candles on the altar — not the short ones, the long ones — and tell Father Renee that I am sick and that he has to send somebody to do my work in church, and also help bring your table and chair to the front door if you can't find somebody else. If worse comes to worse you must bring them yourself, for it is no use staying home and losing also the little money you can earn. Now, go and let me sleep." He laid down again and turned his head toward the wall.

His wife was more surprised than worried. Her husband hadn't been sick for many years and she had never done his chores alone. But she didn't dare bother him with any questions knowing that she could just as well go and find out herself what must be done. Fortunately, she wouldn't have trouble getting the new candles for the sexton always kept them on the second shelf of the side closet.

It was only a small distance to the church because their house was almost built against it. While walking along the short path, she tried to remember what her husband did every morning. She wasn't sure because she sat behind a table just inside the church portal most of the day selling candles, images of saints, and holy water, and he never needed her help. She also did not know how she would bring her heavy table and chair to the church hall.

First, though, she could replace the burnt-out candles standing in front of the image of Mary, take care of the flowers, and dust the altar. That would be a good start.

Without making much noise she went to the altar, changed the candles and made sure that everything looked spick and span. When the new candles were brightly lit, she went to the church entrance at the rear of the church, hoping that some churchgoer would be willing to help her with the table. It was so dark there that it was nearly impossible to see anything, but she was familiar with the church, so she didn't even slacken her pace and hurried past a few closets built against the wall. Yet, it would have been better if she had slowed down somewhat for suddenly she nearly stumbled over what she thought was a broom. When she bent to pick it up, she saw that it wasn't a broom but the legs of a boy who was just as frightened as she. He was scrambling to his feet quickly, and would have run away if her voice hadn't stopped him.

"Hey, boy! Don't run away! I didn't mean to scare you! I'm really pleased to see that you made it to church so early! It doesn't happen too often that a boy is ahead of everybody else. I'll surely tell the sexton who always claims that boys are only good for doing mischief nowadays. What is the matter? You aren't scared of an old woman, are you? What is your name?"

"John, Madame."

"No, I can't remember having seen you before and I always thought that I knew all the people in the neighborhood. It must be that I am getting old, My memory isn't what it used to be. Besides, so many people are moving into the city that it's getting harder and harder to recognize them all. Well, my boy, do you mind helping me a bit? The sexton is sick and he always gives a hand in setting up my table and chair in the portal. I'm not strong enough, you see. I can't do it myself. You are a big boy and if you help me, it won't take more than a few minutes."

"Sure, Madame," John answered hesitantly. He had fallen asleep and had awakened unexpectedly when somebody kicked his legs. He realized that he could hardly run away now, but was determined to disappear as fast as possible.

"Come on, John," she said, and opened the very door that he had been using as a support for his back during the night. "Let's take the table first. Careful, now. Can you carry it alone? Well, well, you really have strong muscles. Don't drop it now! Excellent, just move it against the pillar. Yes, that will do. And now, please get the chair."

While she was talking, John went back, picked up the chair and moved it behind the table without saying a word. The woman thanked him with a flood of words when he was finished and dropped a few small coins into his hand. For a moment he was embarrassed accepting money for such an easy job, but then he remembered how badly he needed it to buy food. After politely thanking her, he rushed out. Surprised that he hurried away, she followed him with her eyes.

"Strange," she thought. "He comes to church for the early Mass, but leaves before it starts. When I see him next time I'll ask why he left so suddenly." Still muttering she seated herself in her chair next to the church door and waited for her first customer.

John stopped running soon and slowed down to a walk. He couldn't help grinning a little when he recalled the surprised look on the face of the old woman.

"Of course, she didn't know me," he thought, amused. She must have taken him for one of the boys of the neighborhood. Anyhow, he had rested well and now the best thing to do was to leave the city as soon as possible. He opened his hand to see how much money she had given him. A few pennies only. It wasn't much but enough to buy some bread, which he needed because he was as hungry as a wolf.

Without knowing it, he approached the center of the city while walking through the streets in search of a bakery. It was amazing how many people were leading cows or carrying merchandise, he thought, but when he arrived unexpectedly at the town square, he suddenly understood the reason. Today was market day!

It was very early in the morning but the market was already in full swing. Lots of people were there already, selling animals or other products. One side of the square was occupied by farmers with their animals: cows, sheep, pigs, chickens, and a few horses. Their wives, on the other side, were busy selling butter, eggs, cheese, and honey. In the rest of the market booths were erected where other articles were sold: knives, clothes, pots, pans, and nearly anything you might think of. There were wrestlers, jugglers, soothsayers, quacks, and also people who tried to make a living by giving one-man shows!

Hesitant about entering, he mixed in with the crowd and amused himself by looking at all the unusual sights, which he had never seen before. It didn't take him long to find a booth where they were selling bread and another one loaded with carrots and apples. It was a pity that he didn't have more money, but at least today he could fill his stomach and even save some food for tomorrow. Chewing an apple, he reflected that it must be possible to make some money by helping somebody.

A few hours later he got his chance. While sauntering along inadvertently to where the cattle were sold, he heard two farmers close a deal. Afterward, one of them invited the other one for a drink to seal the bargain. The man holding the cow was going to refuse the offer, not knowing what to do with the animal, when he saw John.

"Come on, boy, you are just in time! Two nickels for you if you hold onto this cow while I go for a drink! I will be back in a moment!" Without waiting for an answer, he gave the rope to John and disappeared.

Ah, that was something! John felt as happy as could be for this and held the rope tightly. Fortunately, the cow was very quiet and didn't give him any trouble whatsoever. This was a good thing, for it was more than a few minutes before the farmer returned, walking rather unsteadily. He gave John two nickels, took the rope again and walked away.

John, anxious to make more money, didn't lose any time in looking around for other occasions where he could help. Lots of help was needed, and the rest of the day he did all kinds of small jobs. Often he was paid for them and a few times not, but after a few hours he had enough money to buy food for a couple of days.

At the end of the afternoon he decided to leave the city and look for a convenient place in the fields where he could sleep during the nice, warm summer night. It was easy to find the city gates. Many farmers were already going home and he needed only to follow this crowd. Close to one of the gates he again saw his old acquaintance, the farmer who had given him his first job. He must have repeated frequently the drinking performance of that morning because he was drunk. Apparently he had purchased more animals, for three sheep ambled after him with the cow, all tied together with the same rope. This wasn't a very bright idea and had become a source of constant trouble for him and merriment for the bystanders.

The cow apparently disliked having the sheep behind her. Every so often after she had walked a short distance, she would turn around and pull in the opposite direction, with the ridiculous result that the whole cavalcade came to a standstill. After the animals did some rope-pulling without moving, the farmer began to yell and hit them. Suddenly they would jump forward pulling hard on the rope, held tightly by the farmer. Not standing steadily on his legs, he would tumble to the ground and lose the rope. While he struggled to his feet, the animals, feeling that they were free, ran several yards until they found some grass or felt that nobody would catch them. The farmer always managed to grasp the rope again after the animals had calmed down, but then the story repeated itself to the great amusement of everybody.

The farmer, drunk as he was, immediately recognized John, who had stopped when he saw all this going on.

"Boy," he hiccoughed, "you are my big friend, hey? I need help in bringing these animals home. Please give me a hand! Something must be wrong. When they run away I see two cows and when I grab them one always escapes. You know what? If you bring them home, I'll pay you!" With that he went to clap John jovially on his shoulder but missed him completely and nearly fell on the ground again.

John didn't particularly want to go to the house of a drunk farmer. But seeing that the farmer would never make it home without help, he took the guide rope and said shortly, "I'll take them outside the city gate and will wait for you there."

Without even looking to see if the farmer followed him, he took the animals through the streets to the large gate. The animals could feel that John was a good and determined leader and were now easy to lead. As they approached the gate John saw some soldiers sitting leisurely on benches, engrossed in card playing. Two of them were standing, idly leaning against the city wall, scrutinizing the passers-by. Not knowing why the soldiers were observing the crowd, John became frightened. Were they looking for him? For a few moments he wondered if it was safe to pass them, but then ridiculed himself contemptuously for being so easily scared. After all, nobody could know him and they would think that he belonged to the farmer, who walked just behind him. Seeming unconcerned and without paying attention to the soldiers, he walked with his animals through the gate. He was prepared to run away as fast as possible if something should go wrong, but nothing happened.

A safe distance past the gate, he waited for the farmer, who had slouched slowly after him.

"How far is it to your house?" John inquired.

The farmer muttered something about two hours walk. What shall I do? John wondered. Shall I lead the animals all the way or will the farmer do it himself? No, he decided, the farmer couldn't for he was too drunk even to walk straight. So John continued to lead the cow and the sheep. The farmer followed with unsteady steps.

The farmer's drunkenness gradually subsided and he slowly became sober. Sometime later he retook the rope again without saying anything and guided the animals himself. After another hour of walking he left the main road and followed a side path. Finally, John saw a small farmhouse through the bushes. The farmer stopped abruptly and gave John some money.

"Don't tell my wife that I have given you money or that I was drunk," he muttered. "You can have supper with us before you return to the city if you want it."

As soon as they came in full view of the farm, the door opened and a woman came outside scolding and using such awful language that John didn't know what he heard and listened openmouthed. The man ignored the woman and opened a door at the side of the house that lead to the stable. He untied the animals and took them one by one inside. In the meantime, the woman continued her insulting remarks. John understood that she was so angry because the farmer was too late help milk the cows and was drunk, apparently not for the first time.

It was a miracle that her tongue was not completely worn out for her tongue lashing went on for a long time, despite the farmer ignoring her. Hesitantly, John waited to see what would happen for he didn't know if she would invite him to stay or not. After all, the farmer had invited him for supper, although it didn't seem likely that his wife would agree.

After the man had closed the stable door, he turned around, intending to enter the farmhouse. At last, the woman stopped wagging her tongue. She asked her husband, decently enough, who John was. Grumbling, the man replied that John had helped to drive the cattle home, and that he had promised a meal because it wasn't fair to let him walk back to the city for two hours with a hungry stomach. The woman barely waited long enough for the man to stop talking when she, with her shrill voice, began scolding again. Now it was directed to her husband and to John simultaneously. She called her husband a sheephead for inviting John and then told John that she never gave precious food to beggars, but commonly sent them away as she had done to another beggar that very same afternoon. The farmer shrugged his shoulders and went inside the house. Still yelling, his wife followed and slammed the door shut, leaving John standing outside in the cold.

It all happened so fast that at first he was stunned. Then he understood the comical side of this reception and began to laugh so hilariously loud that he barely could stop. Everything was so amusing! That furious woman yelling at them and the indifferent face of her husband, who didn't dare to say anything. He still heard her raging behind the closed doors.

In the meantime, it was getting darker and he had to find a place to sleep before it was impossible to see anything. After a last glance at the door he turned around and already had taken a few steps away from the house when all at once he saw the haystack. Well, that could be an excellent spot for resting! Yet, he first went to the road, suspecting that the woman might keep an eye on him through the windows and it was surely not her business to know his plans.

As soon as he was invisible from the farm, he returned through the fields and with some difficulty managed to sneak unseen up to the haystack. A ladder stood against it, which made it easy to climb. At the top of the hay he began to dig a comfortable, warm hole so that he wouldn't be discovered if somebody climbed the ladder.

Suddenly, while digging in the hay he felt something that gave him the shivers. It was too dark to see what it was, but it felt like a person's leg. He had to overcome a sick, nauseated feeling before he dared to touch it again. Imagine, it could be a beggar who had died in his sleep! After some hesitation, he groped again in the same spot, but now he felt that it was certainly a human leg attached to a body, which was shaking and therefore couldn't be dead!

"How I fooled you," he heard a boy say, laughing. "I wanted to play a trick on you and boy, how scared you were! I felt you shaking all over! What did you think it was?"

John was very much embarrassed. He grinned half-heartedly and changed the subject directly.

"Who are you and what are you doing here? Oh, wait a moment, you must be the boy who was sent away by that woman this afternoon!"

"Yes, of course. What a terrible hag! It was fun hearing her yell at you while I was sitting safely in her haystack."

"Yes," John laughed. "I am sorry for her husband, but I've never heard anybody yell as loudly as she did and she made such faces that I was nearly tickled to death!"

"She looked like a puffing dragon," said the other boy, who didn't want to be outdone by John. Both grinned but didn't dare to laugh loudly, afraid that somebody might hear them.

"I am John. What is your name?"

"I am Camille. Where do you come from?"

"From the south," replied John, trying to be friendly without telling this unknown boy too much. "And I am on my way to Paris."

"That is far. Why are you going there? Do you have any relatives in Paris?"

"Oh, well, I'd like to see Paris for I have heard so much about it," John said evasively. "Let's eat a bit before we go to sleep. Would you like something?" He opened his bag and shared his food with Camille.

"I'm sure happy that you have come," Camille remarked thankfully, after having eaten his fill. "I was very hungry and hadn't any food." John didn't reply. He was afraid that if he asked any questions, Camille would do the same.

Don't worry, he thought to himself. Tomorrow you just leave him and then you'll have nothing more to do with him.

Comfortable and warm in the hay he turned suddenly again to Camille.

"How old are you, Camille?"

"I am thirteen, and you?"

"Sixteen," John said. "Good night!"

A few moments later nothing could be heard except the quiet breathing of the two boys.

John woke up early the next morning. He yawned a few times, rubbed his eyes and sat up in the hay. Looking around, he saw Camille next to him sleeping quietly. He was lying on his back, so that John could see his friendly face. He had dark, curly hair and was incredibly thin, as if he hadn't eaten for weeks.

The best thing to do is to leave without waking him up, John thought. If he discovers that I am a Huguenot he might betray me. Yet, seeing Camille's honest-looking face made him feel sorry for his thoughts. Still, he couldn't risk it, grabbed his bag and crept carefully to the ladder. Unfortunately, he accidently touched Camille slightly when he went by him and that was enough to wake him.

"Hello," Camille said, opening his eyes. "What are you doing so early in the morning?"

"We have to leave directly if we don't want to be caught," John answered, not willing to admit that he had planned to leave without him.

"Alright," Camille said. "I am ready." He stood up, picked up a basket that had served as a pillow, and climbed down the ladder. John followed and a few moments later they were on their way.

When they came to the main road, John asked Camille where he was going. He figured that it would give him a good excuse for leaving Camille by going in the opposite direction. The cheerful expression on Camille's face changed, and he became sad and thoughtful. After a few moments he said, "I really don't know. I have no home anymore and have been just roaming around for a long time. Please, let me go with you. It is much nicer. I don't like being alone. Maybe I can help you. I will be no bother to you. Honest, I promise."

John was surprised to hear his pleading voice. He really was sorry for him and would gladly have accepted his company but was afraid of trusting Camille.

After some thinking John said, "I don't know. I have to go a very large distance and I am used to walking rather fast. I don't think that you, with your short legs, can keep up with me. No, I think it is better not to go together." Camille's eyes filled with tears when he heard John's refusal.

"Can't I go with you at least today?" he asked humbly, in a small voice. When John saw the unhappy look on Camille's face, he felt so much pity for the wretched boy that he didn't dare to say no again. He walked down the road and said "All right then, but hurry up. I want to cover quite a distance today. Are you hungry? We can eat while we are walking, can't we?" He opened his bag and took a few carrots, which he shared with Camille.

Camille's face had already brightened when John said that he could go with him, but when John gave him the carrots he looked as if he had received the most precious gift in his life. In an incredibly short time, the carrots were stored in his stomach. John, seeing how hungry Camille was, asked him how long ago he had eaten and where he had gotten the food. Camille blushed a little and said, "I begged sometimes and if I was very hungry, I stole it from kitchen gardens. I understand that nobody is allowed to steal but I didn't know any other way to stay alive. This week I decided not to steal anymore and therefore I haven't eaten much the last few days." John became more and more sorry for Camille. He opened his bag again and told him to take as much as he wanted. Camille eagerly grasped another piece of bread.

"Where did you get all this delicious food?" he asked with his mouth full, pointing his finger toward John's well-filled bag.

"I was at the market yesterday," John said, "and I earned some money by helping people." Camille didn't reply and for some time the boys walked silently together, both of them wondering how much they could trust each other.

Around noon they became tired for they had walked rather briskly. John proposed to look for a nice, cool, shaded place where they could eat their lunch. It didn't take them long to find just such a place close to the embankment of a little river. After their simple lunch, they had a good rest while they enjoyed the quiet calm of the beautiful scenery.

Camille was the first one to be bored. He suddenly jumped up and said, "How hot it is. Come on, John, let's go for a swim!" Without waiting for an answer he hurriedly undressed and jumped into the small river.

"Is it deep?" John asked. "I can't swim and would rather not drown."

"Oh, no, close to the shore it doesn't even reach my knees."

Hurriedly, John also undressed and carefully stepped into the water. It was true, the water was delightfully cool. Camille, who could swim like an otter, began teasing John and splashed the water so hard around him that he couldn't do anything better than repay him with even larger splashes and so a real water fight started. During one of the most exciting parts of the battle, Camille suddenly stopped. His eyes grew large and he looked attentively at John. Then he rushed forward and yelled, "Oh John, you must also be a Huguenot! I see it. We are . . . mmmpfff." He couldn't finish his sentence because his unexpected rush had made John stumble. He tried his utmost to remain standing and grasped Camille, but both fell head over heels into the water.

After a few moments, they came up again. John was angry. He had only heard half of Camille's shouting. Camille, still laughing, was nearly choking. Both began spitting water for neither one of them had closed his mouth under water.

Camille yelled, laughed, and wept all at the same time.

"You are a Huguenot and so am I! Now we must stick together for we need each other." He danced around in the water and kept singing in a loud, excited voice, "Now I have a friend."

"Hush," John warned. He at last understood what was going on. "Hush, keep your mouth shut. Do you want somebody to hear you? Be quiet, boy! If anyone hears you we both will be sent to prison. Stop it now!" Impatiently he shook Camille's hand away and went to the shore to dress himself. Camille, frightened by John's remark, quieted down and followed him. After they had dressed again, they sat close together in the shade of a tree, refreshed by their swim.

"Now you must tell me first, John, who you really are and why you are wandering around. Where do your parents live? Why are you going to Paris or was that just an excuse? Now we can stay together, right, John?"

He didn't have to ask twice. John told him everything. He talked about his father who was on the galleys, of his mother who had passed away, and how he planned to free Manette so they could run away to Holland. He told him also about his difficult trip, about his adventure within the coach and in the church, about Mother Rosette and everything that had happened. Camille listened attentively. He didn't say much, just, "Yes, I will go with you. I have no home where I can stay. You are right, the only thing to do is to go to Holland. Of course, we have to go to Paris first, but that makes no difference at all."

11

CAMILLE'S STORY

Both boys were silent for a long time after John had finished his story. Then Camille, shyly looking toward the river, began to relate his adventures.[12]

"John, you're blessed to have parents who both love the Lord, even though your father is on the galleys and your mother is not here anymore. My parents are still alive in Montaigne, but I'm not that fortunate. Your father refused to return to the Roman Church, but my father and mother were not so courageous. They gave in and became 'new converts.' I had to attend Mass every morning, and of course, we had to partake in all kinds of other idolatries. At home, Dad was different. He must have been sorry that he had returned to the Roman Church, and in the beginning he taught me secretly from the Bible, insisting that I memorize many verses. I had to go to the instruction classes given by the priest. In the beginning nearly all the boys called me a heretic and refused to play with me. However, soon I made some new friends who were also sons of 'new converts.'

"A few years ago we found a cave in the woods and began using it as a meeting place. It became a kind of routine to come together every Saturday for Bible reading and Psalm singing. Gastro, who had no father, always brought his mother's Bible and the few times he couldn't come, we recited Bible verses that we had memorized!

"I became Gastro's best friend and often visited his house. He had a nice mother, who taught us a lot of Bible stories, all of them beautiful. She also told us that the Huguenots were often persecuted, and how they were willing to give their lives for Jesus' sake.

"After those stories I always felt embarrassed that Mom and Dad had recanted and that we had become Romanists again. Very often I wondered if I couldn't do anything to change it, but didn't know what. I wasn't the only one who worried, for last winter my friends also began to talk about their parents and how wrong they

---

[12] This is a true story that happened in 1699 in a village called Monteils.

were. We were all afraid that they would go to hell if they didn't repent. After many discussions we felt that God wanted us to be an example for our parents to encourage them to serve Christ by leaving the Roman Church.

"We agreed to go to church early Sunday morning and to sing Psalms. We hoped that maybe they would join us and renounce the Roman Church. It didn't work. We were chased away and they were visited by the priest. He warned them severely. He thought that they had made us do it. When I came home that evening Dad spanked me very hard, indeed. I wasn't allowed to see my friends any more and he told me that it would be worse for me if I did it again. All my pleading that he would leave the Roman Church was in vain for he was so scared that he didn't even listen.

"My father watched me closely the next Saturday, which made it impossible to leave the house, but the following week I managed to sneak out to our cave. We were all very disappointed that it hadn't worked out, but agreed to try it again the next day. Our parents might then understand that we were really serious. Gastro was the only one who refused to come, for his mother didn't think it was right and he didn't want to be disobedient.

"The next day, as soon as we began to sing, a group of armed men appeared and put us in prison. Afterward, I heard that our parents had been jailed as well and were interrogated by the priest. Obviously, they insisted they were innocent, but he didn't believe them. After they were dismissed, we were brought in. He warned us that we would be severely punished unless we admitted that our parents had made us do it. We explained that they weren't to blame because we hadn't told them and that we were singing the Psalms because we desired to praise God. I don't know if we convinced him, but I think we did for he changed the subject and demanded that we say we were sorry for our conduct and promise that we would never do it again. This, of course, we couldn't do and so he had us returned to prison.

"That very same night, some of our group and I escaped. Gastro, who wasn't caught because he hadn't participated in our singing, came secretly to the prison and managed to remove the few iron bars in the window opening. We began to climb through it and a few of us were already outside when the guard found out. They tried to catch us, but we scattered in different directions and I outran them. However, I had lost the other ones. I didn't dare return to the village and so I have just wandered since that night.[13]

"I slept in haystacks and dry ditches, and begged or stole food. Last week I became sorry about my stealing and tried hard not to do it anymore. Well, you know how hungry I was when you found me in the haystack. I'm sure that you must have been sent by God for I have prayed for many weeks that He would let me meet a Huguenot who could help me. I didn't know what to do or where to go. At times I thought that it might be better to return to my parents and accept the consequences. Last night I was really desperate for I thought that nobody cared about me anymore, but now everything has turned out well."

He waited a few moments, deep in thought, and then said, "John, I am so thankful that I want to thank God for it. Will you pray with me?"

John didn't answer but nodded and the two boys knelt together in the grass and gave thanks to their Father Who had brought them together when they needed it most. They didn't forget to pray for all Huguenots who were persecuted, and then they asked His guidance so that they might escape with Manette to Holland.

The boys were quiet for a long time afterward. Both were absorbed in their own thoughts. Camille was thinking how good it was that he had met John. John was also thankful for he realized how much easier his escape had been than Camille's. At last he said, "Well, it seems to me rather important to figure out how to get to Paris, since we have agreed to stick together. Let's see first how much food and money we have." He opened his bag and they scrutinized its contents carefully. There was enough food for several days if they didn't eat too much. Besides, John also had some money. Camille had nothing and his basket was empty, which he demonstrated by turning it over and shaking it. John suddenly saw how well the basket had been woven and asked Camille how he got hold of it. Camille told him proudly that his father, who was a basket-maker, had made it and given it to him as a birthday present. He liked it so much that he always took it with him, even when he escaped from jail.

---

[13] The other boys fled and with other young people formed a religious group. In two villages they forced their way into the Roman Church and made a bonfire with the images. When soldiers tried to catch them, the youngsters found a hiding place deep in the forest where they continued their worship services for many years.

"If you want one," he added, "I can make one for you because Dad taught me how to do it."

"You can make baskets?" John asked, amazed.

"Just the small ones, for my hands aren't strong enough to bend the larger branches."

"Hurrah! In that case we won't be hungry anymore, for we can easily make enough money to purchase our food!" Excitedly, he explained to the dumfounded Camille that they could make small baskets and sell them to farmers or to the people in the cities.

"It will give us enough money for food. You better believe it! It helps a lot not to have to worry about such things! By the way, what materials do you need for basket-making?"

"Well, willow branches and a sharp knife."

"You know what we'll do? Tomorrow we'll go along this river which is in the right direction, anyway. We'll find a spot with willows and stay a few days. You can make as many baskets as possible. Then we'll go on our way and trade them in for money or food. Two boys selling baskets are beyond suspicion. We aren't beggars and don't need to steal!"

It made Camille happy to know that he could be of some help to his friend.

"Oh, yes. Willows always grow near water and they may even be very close by," he remarked. "Let's look for them right now. It isn't dark yet and we have enough time to explore the banks in this area."

"An excellent idea!" John said, "If you go in that direction, I will go this way. Remember to be back here before it becomes dark, though. It's warm enough for sleeping outside, and I don't think that it will rain tonight."

Just before dark the boys were back again. Camille hadn't found a thing, but John had good news.

"Further down is a kind of swamp area where all kinds of willows grow," he told Camille. "It is hard to find in the dark, but let's go there early tomorrow morning. It's an excellent place and we can stay as long as needed without anybody seeing us. Maybe you can also teach me how to make baskets, which will speed things up."

They had a good night's rest and awoke just before daybreak by the chill in the air. Sometimes shivering with cold, they began to walk and had already gone a good distance when the sun came above the horizon. The warm sunshine made walking so pleasant that it was a kind of disappointment to arrive at the swamp so soon. It was surrounded by willow trees and very much suited for their plans. Without much ado, Camille got the knife, cut a small supply of branches and began, diligently, to make a basket while John watched him. Every time when the supply of branches became exhausted, John cut new ones so that Camille didn't have to interrupt his weaving. They made quite a lot of progress that very first day.

For two days and nights they stayed in that lonely spot. It was a nice, peaceful period. Every day they worked as long as it was light enough to see the weaving. Initially only Camille made the baskets, but in a very short time John had learned to make the simple ones by watching Camille, who loved to teach. Of course, they chatted quite a lot during the basket-making. Yet, the best time of the day was after supper at night. Then they put away their baskets and their knives and talked about the Bible. It became clear that John knew far more about it than Camille. His parents had told him very little, partly because they were afraid of the priest, but also because they never had learned very much themselves.

The second night after the boys had lain in the grass for a long time doing nothing but watching the beautiful stars, Camille suddenly turned to John and said, "I'm always wondering why the Church in France has disappeared. Of course, the Roman Church is everywhere, but I don't count that one because it's a false church. I mean why was it allowed to destroy the Huguenot Church, and why don't we have ministers to preach the gospel to us and also to the Romanists so that they will repent? Is it true what the priest told me once, that barely any Huguenots are left? Is it possible that in a few more years nobody will know they ever existed? Why do Churches exist in other countries and why did we never succeed in building a Church here?"

John waited a few moments before he replied. He realized only now how little Camille really knew of the Church. As a matter of fact, he also felt these questions to be rather difficult. However, by recalling as much as possible what his mother had told him he felt sure that he could at least give some answer to these questions.

"I really don't know where to start, Camille, for there is so much to tell about our Church that we could talk for hours. My mother wasn't born in Lisieux. She came from the Cevennes, and even at present, thousands of Huguenots still live there.[14] When she married, she came to Lisieux where my father also was converted. My mother knew the Bible much better than my father and knew also a lot about the history of the Church. She told me a lot about it. She mentioned that I should never forget the year 1517. In that year God used a monk named Luther to re-form His Church. However, the priests and the Pope didn't like it and excommunicated him. Happily, it didn't stop the Reformation because Luther, with other Christians who agreed with him, formed the true Church of Christ.

"The writings of Luther were quickly known in France. A few years later a Frenchman, John Calvin, was converted. He was an arduous Christian and his whole life was dedicated to the service of Christ. God used him — a very capable, learned man — to teach the Church to listen to the Bible again. In his sermons and writings he gave a true and beautiful explanation of the Holy Scripture. My mother was always very sorry that she didn't have any of his books. My grandfather owned two of them and often read large sections to her when she was still a little girl. It was *The Institutes of the Christian Religion* and the other book was an explanation of one of the books in the Bible, I think of Paul's letter to the Romans. Anyhow, this man Calvin became very influential in France. He had to flee to Geneva where he spent the rest of his life, as far as I know. Yet, very soon a great many people in France listened to him and gladly accepted his teachings. Mother told me that in those times the majority of the people in France were Huguenots.

"However, the Pope and the King didn't like this at all. A few years later thousands and thousands of Huguenots were murdered in Paris and the rest of the country during one night, called Bartholomew night. Mother once said that she had heard that at least forty thousand had been killed.

"Fortunately, later another king gave freedom of religion, and the Huguenots lived in peace for a short time. Persecution and religious

---

[14] Half of the population of the Cevennes, a mountainous area deep in the south of France, consisted of Waldenses and Huguenots (approximately 340,000). The persecution in this area was atrocious. These Christians defended themselves against the soldiers of King Louis XIV in the famous War of the Camisards (1702-1704). King William of Orange used all his political power in an effort to halt their suffering. Queen Mary, his wife, gave huge sums of money for financial support.

wars have been very common in our country. Our present king, King Louis has been — and still is — trying to liquidate the Huguenots during his long reign. However, the Huguenots have always known how to suffer for the sake of Christ. Many of them have been killed, but they were even singing Psalms on the scaffold where they were put to death. My mother told me that their suffering and death often brought many other people to Christ.

"I am amazed that you don't know that in the past more than eight hundred churches existed in France and that our first synod[15] was already held in 1559. Even today France has many Churches, and quite a few ministers are preaching the Word of God secretly.

"Yes, Camille, even though we don't know any other Huguenots, we need not become desperate, for the Lord has promised never to forsake us. Sometimes in history the Church has been so small that nearly nobody knew about it, but the Bible teaches that the Church will remain on the earth until the Day of Judgment. Then Jesus Christ will return to judge the living and the dead."

For a short time both were quiet but then Camille sighed and said, "I would like to know as much as you. Everything would be much easier then." Nothing more was said and very soon they were sleeping peacefully.

The next morning they left the willow grove and continued their journey. They had made nine baskets and figured that was good enough for a start.

---

[15] A synod is an ecclesiastical meeting in which the local churches are represented by some of their office bearers.

12

SUPPORT FROM
IN THE FISHING CAT

It would hardly be possible to find a better location for the small inn, which stood in one of the most crowded sections of Paris. It was so near to the city gates that travelers could find it easily. Yet, the noise and clamor of the traffic didn't disturb its quiet neighborhood for it was also far enough away from the main street. The building didn't look very impressive but its red outer walls and bright green door, which had been painted recently, gave it a neat and clean appearance. Swaying over the door was a sign with a clumsy drawing of a kind of nondescript animal with a fishing rod in one of its paws and a large fish at the end of the line. Painted below the drawing were odd, irregular letters that spelled, *In The Fishing Cat.*

Inside, the inn was rather quiet. There were no customers and the innkeeper was sitting peacefully in the corner of the room with his legs stretched out on another chair. He looked like a jolly fellow, not very old — maybe forty years — with a waistline so big that, standing up straight, he couldn't even see his toes. He had an honest face and small, alert eyes, which revealed that it was not very easy to fool him.

He had been sitting for at least an hour, enjoying the usual quiet time in the morning. It was Friday again, which meant that he wouldn't see his wife for another few hours. She was a devout church-goer and always considered Friday to be an exceptionally good day for being in church as long as possible to accumulate as many good works as she could.

Yes, he reflected, I have done well during all the years I have been in business. He had started as a sailor when he was young and had traveled everywhere. His earnings had been low, especially in the beginning, but he hadn't needed very much either, so he always managed to put aside some of his wages. His savings had increased a lot by helping with some well-planned smuggling. As soon as it became too dangerous he quit and found a simple job in Paris. He didn't have much money, but after his wedding he discovered, to his pleasant surprise, that his wife had also saved a little, just enough to buy this inn. He had never regretted doing it.

His wife kept everything spick and span, and he, also, liked to see everything immaculate. She was an excellent cook. His belly was good evidence. Besides, she had brought him a large number of customers because she was a good Roman Catholic and many nuns were friendly with her. It made the inn very popular for everyone who belonged to the clergy. It was common for priests and monks to drop in for a drink. In all of Paris, his inn was outstanding because it was the 'clergy' inn. He didn't mind it having that name. As long as he could make a living, he didn't care to whom he sold his spirits. He went to church once in awhile because his wife insisted and because it gave him a better name, which was good for his business. Yet, for the rest . . . he didn't care a penny and believed precious little of the traditions and beliefs of the Roman Church.

Suddenly the door opened and two boys walked in. Both looked healthy and sun tanned and carried a load of baskets on their backs. The innkeeper, Jacob was his name, saw instantly that they didn't belong to his regular customers.

"They must be basket-makers from the country," he guessed. He always considered everybody who didn't live in Paris as coming from the country. While he made these observations the boys — John and Camille — seated themselves at one of the tables.

It had taken them a long time to get to Paris. they hadn't encountered any special difficulties, but it was a large distance and they had covered it without hurrying. The idea of making and selling baskets had proven to be excellent. Very soon they found that the wives of most farmers could not pay for the baskets, for money was scarce, but all of them were very willing to pay with a good meal. The only place for the boys to get money was in the larger villages or small cities where the well-to-do women were pleased to pay a few pennies for the baskets. After all, they were very handy to carry things when going to and from the market.

Gradually they had also lost their fear of priests and soldiers. Common sense told them that they were unknown so far away from their homes and that it was unlikely that anyone would guess they were Huguenots, provided they didn't give themselves away. With money in their pockets and by freely, but carefully mixing with other people, they had become rather independent. As a result, they hadn't been hungry anymore, except at one occasion when they had sold all their baskets for meals without having any money at all. Their search for proper branches and then making the new baskets had taken several days. During this time they didn't have any food. But they had survived and the ordeal hadn't been too bad, after all. Afterward, they had even succeeded in saving some money and therefore considered themselves to be rich, indeed!

It had been rather simple to find *In The Fishing Cat* where Mother Rosette's son was living. They asked directions for its location and were told that monks and nuns loved to go there. Somewhat suspicious of an inn with such a reputation, they had planned that John would order a meal first and then begin a conversation with the innkeeper so that they could find out what kind of man he was. They felt they couldn't be too careful if they wanted to remain at liberty and free Manette.

A few moments later, Jacob pulled his feet from the chair, stood up and lazily stretched himself. After a quick look through the window, he went to the boys and asked what he could serve them. John, always less shy than Camille, said that they wanted to have a good meal, chicken would be best if available. Jacob's eyes opened wide with surprise and he replied curtly that they didn't serve meat on Friday. Friday was a fasting day and good Roman Catholics were not supposed to eat meat on such days.

Both boys turned scarlet for they knew it to be true, but had completely forgotten which day of the week it was. It was surely embarrassing to give yourself away with the very first words you speak to a stranger!

"Oh, yes. I forgot that it is Friday today," said John. "Maybe you could bring us some bread, butter and a few fried eggs. And also something to drink, please." Jacob looked at John with a puzzled expression on his face and gave the impression that he intended to say something. Apparently he changed his mind quickly for he shrugged his shoulders, turned around and disappeared into the kitchen.

While he was preparing the meal, he had his own thoughts about the unusual behavior of the boys. It was strange and uncommon for a good Roman Catholic to forget that it was Friday. It could happen, but it was certainly suspicious that the boys had blushed so much and looked so guilty.

Anyway, he didn't care. As long as they paid their bill, he would serve them, although they were fortunate that his wife hadn't heard it.

In the meantime, the boys had a whispered discussion. They were aware that the innkeeper didn't trust them after their blunder. Camille suggested they leave the inn, before the man returned, but John insisted that they should find out first if he was the son of Mother Rosette. It was always possible to run away, he thought. They were sitting close to the door and could, if needed, leave the baskets behind. It was worth the risk. They were still talking about it when Jacob returned with plates loaded with bread and fried eggs. While he was placing them in front of the boys, John asked suddenly, "Do you ever hear anything from Mother Rosette?"

The man was so amazed that he nearly dropped his serving tray.

"What? My old mother? You have seen her? How do you happen to know her?"

"Well, I stayed with her for more than a week." John told Jacob briefly what had happened, although he didn't give any reason for his roaming around.

Obviously, Jacob wanted to know everything about her and was very happy that he could talk with somebody who had seen her recently.

Suddenly he stopped in the middle of a sentence.

"Wait a moment," he said. "Now I understand what kind of people you are. You must be Huguenots! You didn't remember about the fasting on Friday and besides, you came from the south where a lot of them live! As a matter of fact, I am convinced that you would not have stayed with my mother if it hadn't been a good hiding place. Not many people dare to enter her cottage. They are afraid and think that she is a witch!"

John was surprised to hear how much Jacob had guessed, but didn't want to mention that they were fleeing. He looked at his host and saw that he had an honest, shrewd face. Maybe he could convince him not to ask more questions!

"Mother Rosette didn't ask me anything because she felt that as long as she didn't know me well she couldn't be held responsible for giving shelter to a Huguenot. Can't you do the same here?"

"No way! We aren't living in the country. I don't like to lose my inn and everything I have because I have given you boys a place to sleep! Besides, you can't sleep here without my wife knowing it and she is a devoted Romanist. It would be disastrous for you and me if she found out who you are. Still, I don't want you to go away today for you must tell me much more about my old mother!"

Glad that Jacob sounded so reasonable, John replied, "I would love to stay because we intend to spend some time in Paris, anyway."

"Alright, then. I have an idea how to get a good sleeping place for you but I cannot take you there now because my wife may come home any moment. A few monks often come around noon to drink a glass of wine before they eat their dry meal in the monastery. You just sit down here and keep quiet! As soon as more people are around I will demand the money you owe me. You must tell me that you haven't any. I will use it as an excuse to throw you out on the street. But tonight, as soon as it is dark, you must wait for me outside. Take care that nobody sees you. When I leave the inn, I will carry a lantern and you must follow me. I will take you to a safe sleeping place and tomorrow we can talk some more."

The boys didn't exactly understand what he intended to do and began asking questions. However, Jacob only laughed and waved their questions away.

"Don't worry. Your part is very easy. Just make sure that you are waiting outside the door tonight and don't be late!"

Laughing he turned around and seated himself again in the same corner where he had sat before. Once in a while he looked with a smile at the boys but when he heard footsteps a short time later, he pretended to look bored.

The door opened and his wife entered, accompanied by two nuns. They glanced quickly around and disappeared through a door in the rear of the room. Soon his wife came back, filled a few glasses with wine, and took them to the back room with her. The boys didn't look up and tried not to draw her attention for they were rather afraid of her. They just waited to see what else would happen. Soon the street door opened again and a few monks walked in. Monks were supposed to eat very moderately, but these monks apparently didn't accept such ideas for they were as fat as pigs. They seated themselves, and each ordered a glass of beer. Gradually more and more people walked in. True, most of them belonged to the clergy and only a few common people entered. Half an hour later the room was well filled. At that moment the innkeeper, who was busy serving all his customers, turned to the boys and said, "You had better pay me now. We do not have much room and other customers are waiting. Order something or pay me and leave!"

John, who had used his time to think out the role he had to play said, hesitantly, "I am sorry, Sir, but we have no money. We hoped that you would accept a pair of these beautiful baskets as payment. We are poor boys and this is all we have."

Although John and Camille were somewhat prepared for the scene that followed, they were still taken by surprise by the consequences of their request. Jacob became so angry that it sounded as if a bomb exploded. He was, apparently, very strong. He lifted John and Camille up at the same time and carried them as two small children to the door. The boys, really afraid now, struggled to get loose but Jacob kicked the door open and threw them both onto the street. It didn't happen in silence, either! Jacob yelled so loudly that all customers and passers-by stopped to listen to the venom he spat on the boys. After a few minutes, he went inside again and banged the door behind him.

Nobody showed any sympathy for the boys. Everybody looked with disapproval at the two rascals who dared to eat in a decent inn without a penny in their pockets to pay for it.

They scrambled up, picked up their baskets, which Jacob had thrown after them, and ran away, ducking into the first alley they saw.

In the next street where they dared to walk again, John remarked, "I wish that fellow hadn't treated us as a bag of garbage. I feel broken all over, and it's no fun to keep walking all afternoon. How do you feel?"

"Terrible," Camille answered. "But what are we going to do? Do you think we can trust him? Maybe he will turn us over to his friends, the monks!"

John reflected a moment. "Yes, I think that we can trust him. After all, he treated us decently enough, although he could have handled us a little more tenderly. I think that it will be best if we tell him everything so that he can help us or at least give us some advice."

Camille wasn't so sure about it and they discussed it extensively while strolling through the streets. They were much impressed by the city. The rows of houses seemed to have no end and the houses themselves were of many different sizes and styles. They saw very small houses that resembled sheds more than living quarters but also large, beautiful mansions. There were small churches and also a huge cathedral.

The streets were crowded and a great variety of carriages were in the main streets. The carriage drivers didn't stop for people, and several times the boys had to jump aside to avoid being run over.

The carriages were richly attired and often equipped with a board behind the enclosed seating part on which the servants of the owners stood, wearing beautiful clothes with expensive wigs on their heads. The boys became more and more impressed with the busy and luxurious lives of these people but also with the horrible poverty they saw everywhere.

In the small side streets, alleys, and lanes poor people were crowded together in dirty buildings and the children, playing in the streets, had a pale, unhealthy color. A great number of beggars and invalids were asking for food or money. Most of them sat in front of the churches hoping to receive alms from the pious church-goers.

No, the city of Paris, the mighty capital of France where they had arrived at last, didn't make a good impression at all. It didn't bother them, though, because they had far more serious worries. How could they ever find Manette in this crowd? John hadn't seen her for more than two years. During that time he knew she had changed considerably. Besides, there were so many people in this city that it seemed far easier to find a single needle in a haystack than a tiny girl in such a crowd. They discussed their problem and tried to concoct a way to find her but all their deliberations were in vain. They couldn't find any solution!

At last Camille said, "I'm sure that she has to go to church every day. It seems to me that the only thing left is to watch the church goers from every church a few days. It would be rather strange if we wouldn't find her by simply watching the people."

Even though it sounded like a good idea, both boys felt their courage failing them. They had already discovered so many churches in this city that it would have taken many weeks to visit them all, which would be quite impossible. They didn't have enough money to stay such a long time in Paris unless they could earn some.

At sunset the boys were standing in front of *In The Fishing Cat* in spite of the difficulty they had in locating the inn again. Just across from the inn on the other side of the street they saw a small niche in which they could stand and keep an eye on the inn door.

It was getting so dark that they began to wonder if the innkeeper had forgotten them when the door opened and somebody with a lantern stepped outside. Most of the other people had left the inn without a lantern so they were rather sure it must be the innkeeper this time.

When he lifted the lantern somewhat so that the light fell over his face and the boys could recognize him their doubts disappeared.

It was not difficult to follow him for he moved slowly along the street, although they had to be careful not to stumble in the dark. Soon he turned a corner and continued a short distance until he came to an alley that was so narrow that they couldn't walk next to each other. It was a dead-end street, closed off by a door. Jacob halted in front of it and waited for the boys to come up to him while he took a key from his pocket. When the boys were close, he opened the door and entered the building. They followed him, and he locked the door again as soon as they were inside.

They stood in a small space, which apparently had been used as a stable. It could easily accommodate three horses, but it didn't seem to be used anymore. Across from the spot where they were standing was another much larger door. On their right they saw a step ladder going up to the next floor.

Without saying a word, the innkeeper climbed the ladder and the boys did the same. This floor appeared to be an attic, nearly empty, but with some straw in one corner. Jacob placed the lantern on the floor, piled some straw together and seated himself comfortably.

When he saw the boys silently watching him, he began to laugh and said, "You both look as if you have arrived unexpectedly in a robber's den. Isn't this a good place to stay tonight? Tomorrow I will bring you both a good breakfast and after that you will be free to go to any place you want. Come on, don't be shy! Get yourselves some straw and sit down. Then we can talk. My wife thinks that I have gone to visit a friend and doesn't expect me home before midnight. I have brought something to drink too."

He placed two bottles of wine beside him.

"By the way, do you know where you are? We are just behind *In The Fishing Cat*. The large door downstairs opens into the court of my inn. The previous owner used these stables for the horses of his guests, but we don't take overnight guests and are not using this building. Now, first I want to have a drink and then you must tell me more about my old mother."

The boys were soon at ease with this friendly man. John told him about his stay with Mother Rosette and answered all Jacob's questions. At last he mentioned that he had a gold piece, a Louis d'Or, that Mother Rosette had suggested that Jacob might perhaps change it into smaller coin. Jacob didn't reply at first but just sat thinking.

At last he said, "John, I am glad that you weren't afraid of my mother and that you have been a help to her. You mentioned that she wanted you to stay and take my place. That means that she really liked you. I think that I will help you as much as possible. But you can't expect me to run any risk unless I know your whole story. The very moment I saw you, I realized that you both were Huguenots, but I don't understand what you are doing here in Paris. If you try to flee the country you should have gone south to Marseille, and from there you could have gone safely by boat. You had better tell me everything and then I will try to help, provided the risk is not too great. I am sure this is exactly what my mother would like me to do, and for that reason she sent you to me with your gold piece."

John understood at once that Jacob's demand was reasonable and therefore told him briefly everything that had happened. In the beginning he was a little hesitant, but gradually he told more and more until Jacob knew everything. Also Camille related his story. After he had finished it was quiet for several minutes.

"It's far more difficult than I had expected, boys. I thought that by giving you some money I could put you on the road again, but now I see that helping you more or less includes that I have to give a hand in finding and freeing your little sister. That, of course, I cannot do. It is something you have to do yourself. I think that right now you cannot expect more from me than to let you use this sleeping place as long as you need it. Every morning I will bring you food or better yet I'll do it in the dark at night. Do you know where your sister is living?"

They had to confess that they didn't. Hearing this unexpected reply, Jacob couldn't help laughing.

"Do you mean to tell me that you are going to search all the houses in Paris to find your little sister? You have no idea how large Paris is, I'm afraid. Besides, it will be absolutely impossible for you to find her when she has been sent to a nunnery. I admire your courage, but I think that you're wasting your time looking for her. If I were you I would leave before winter sets in. It is already September and in another six or eight weeks it will be too cold to sleep in haystacks. Believe me, the best thing is to give it up!"

Both boys protested and replied that they wanted at least to give it a try. At last, Jacob said thoughtfully, "Maybe I can find out from my wife about her. You never know, although I never heard her mention the name Manette. How old is she and what does she look like?"

It was rather late when the boys had told everything they knew about Manette, and Jacob had to leave for home. He gave John the key to the door, took the lantern and went downstairs.

"I can use the other door," he said, "and I'll put your food there."

The boys remained behind, glad that they had found a helper although they were not very much encouraged. At last Camille remarked, "John, don't you think that God has helped us all along? Why wouldn't He help also to find Manette? Isn't it written in the Bible 'Ask and it will be given unto thee'? I think that we should start our search tomorrow. We can watch the churchgoers and at the same time sell our baskets at the houses in the neighborhood. Let's not be discouraged but continue to trust the Lord."

13

CAMILLE FINDS MANETTE

Two weeks later, Camille was walking through the streets alone. They had watched the churchgoers every day for Manette, but to no avail. They had found no trace of her. At night they still slept in the stable of the innkeeper, who had daily given them more food than they could eat, and gradually he had become a good friend. He had even asked his wife if she knew the whereabouts of a little girl called Manette, but she didn't. No one seemed to know where she was.

At last Jacob advised them to sell baskets from door to door. He told them where they could find branches outside the city to make new ones. They had been selling baskets for many a long day, but still hadn't discovered Manette. Camille had even asked little children more than once if they knew a girl named Manette. Once he thought he had found her! A little girl told him that she knew somebody with that name. He had promised her a penny if she would show him where that girl was living. She did, but it was again another disappointment, for it turned out that it was a girl of at least sixteen years old.

Today John had gone to cut more branches and left Camille alone. He was still looking for Manette, but realized that he had far less chance without John because he didn't even know what she looked like. The only thing for him to do was to ask for a girl named Manette and hope for the best. He didn't expect to be more successful than the other days, though, but he didn't want to stay in the stable either. So he had taken the last two baskets and left. But where should he go? He was sick and tired of going from house to house. Why shouldn't he go to the vegetable market? He turned around and after a few minutes reached the market, where he soon was mingling with all kinds of people. He aimlessly strolled around between the stands with vegetables. Every once in a while he stopped to listen to the boisterous sales talk of the merchants, which he thought to be very funny.

At last, being rather tired of walking, he looked around for a place to rest. He was close to the center of the market, near a large community waterpump. It was surrounded by a low wall made of large stones. Heavy iron rings, used for tying up horses, were attached to it. He seated himself on the wall and watched the people who came to drink or just past by.

It was fun to see how different they all looked. Most of them were shabbily dressed women who, after a quick glance around, knew directly where they could get the best bargains. They were experts in negotiating and nearly always succeeded in getting far lower prices than the merchants initially demanded. Once he saw a servant following a somewhat better dressed woman. She must surely be the cook in a large, rich house for she purchased such a large quantity of food that the servant could barely carry it. A great number of maidservants, who bought less, thought it also below their dignity to carry their own purchases. A whole flock of small boys running freely around in the crowd kept an eye on them hoping that they would be asked to carry their shopping bags and earn a few pennies.

Toward the end of the afternoon, he saw a large, surly looking woman coming in his direction followed by a poorly dressed, thin girl, who was carrying a big basket filled to the brim with a great number of different vegetables. He couldn't help seeing them because the girl was such a sorry sight. The basket was far too heavy for her and had such an odd shape that it was awkward to carry. Since the girl was not able to lift the basket high enough, she had to drag it along beside her. She looked tired and was panting hard. Yet, the woman didn't seem to care for she kept going without helping her. Every time the girl stopped a moment to catch her breath the woman berated her vigorously. She certainly doesn't look nice, Camille reflected, becoming angry. Drinking a bottle of vinegar every day wouldn't make her look more disgusting! She had a glum, unpleasant face, indeed! No doubt about it. The corners of her mouth were drawn down as if she had never laughed in her whole life, and her lips were so tightly pinched together that they seemed bloodless!

When they were close to Camille, the woman told the girl to stop and wait for her while she did some more shopping.

"Mind, Mary, you keep standing here and make sure that nobody steals from your basket. If anything is missing when we come home, you'll pay for it as sure as my name is Juliette. And don't eat from it, either, I warn you!" Without waiting for a reply, she went back to the market stalls again.

The girl remained silent, but a few large tears slid down her face while she kept standing patiently, waiting for the woman to return. Camille moved up a bit to make room for her beside him and said, "I think you are tired. You'd better sit down to rest and if you want, I'll help you keep an eye on the basket." The girl, frightened, looked up and just shook her head.

It was never very easy to discourage Camille, especially not now for he was really interested in her. So he tried again, "Your name is Mary, right? Who is that woman? Is she your mother? Come on, don't be a milksop, just sit down for a moment and let's be friends."

Thankful for these nice words, the girl turned to him and said, "That woman is the maidservant in the house where I work. If she sees me sitting down or talking with somebody, they will beat me at home. Please, leave me alone for otherwise everything will be worse for me."

Camille didn't know what to say anymore for he certainly didn't want to make life harder for the girl and therefore kept silent. Suddenly, it struck him that he must have seen her somewhere for her face looked familiar, maybe she resembled somebody he knew. He tried hard to remember when that might have been, but hadn't the faintest idea. Maybe we saw her when we sold our baskets, he thought, for we saw so many people!

While he was thinking about it, he got the idea that he could at least ask her if she knew Manette. He turned again to her and said, "Mary, my friend and I are looking for a girl of your age. Her name is Manette. Did you ever hear of that girl?"

An astonished smile crept slowly across the girl's face and she blushed from pure surprise.

"My name is Manette, but I don't think that you are looking for me."

"But that woman called you Mary," Camille exclaimed, amazed. "Yes, she and everyone else in that terrible house where I live calls me that, but my mother always called me Manette."

Camille, hardly believing his own ears, jumped up in surprise. "But then you must be John's little sister. Are you from Lisieux?"

"Yes, and I have a brother John, but I don't know you."

"Manette, for weeks we have searched for you and we have come to . . ." Suddenly he stopped. Just in time he saw the woman appearing behind the girl and he didn't want her to hear what he said.

Unexpectedly, the woman slapped the girl across the face and said, "You know that you are not allowed to talk with boys. Pick up your basket and we will show you at home how we teach disobedient girls."

The girl, in sudden fright, bent over the basket and tried to hide the tears streaming down her face.

The woman scanned Camille from head to toe and said, "You know that girl? What business have you to talk to her? You better come with us so that we can find out who you are!" She tried to grab his arm but Camille easily dodged her and ran away. He didn't go very far, though, just far enough to hide behind people so he could follow the woman and Manette. In his happy excitement he bumped into many people, but he didn't care that they scolded him as long as he could keep an eye on Manette.

Now, at last, he knew why her face appeared to be so familiar. She looked exactly like John! Everybody could see that they are brother and sister! But having found her was not enough. Now he must discover where she lived and he was determined to find out very fast! He followed the woman and the girl at a distance without them knowing.

To his great surprise, they stopped in front of a rather small house, only a few streets away from the inn. The woman opened the front door and both went in.

He walked past the house three times to make sure that he could find it again. After that, he considered very carefully what his next step should be. He hoped that John would be back early so that he didn't have to wait long to tell him the good news. Without losing any time, he went straight to the stable, but found to his great disappointment that John hadn't returned yet.

John didn't come back until just before dark. He was elated when Camille told him the good news and asked many questions, which Camille, of course, couldn't answer. After all, he had seen Manette for only a short time and couldn't even remember all the details of their brief conversation. John insisted that they should go to the house immediately because he wanted to see for himself where Manette was living. It was too dark to distinguish the house from its surroundings, but John was happy just to see the walls behind which Manette slept.

When they returned to the stable, they found that Jacob was waiting. Nowadays, he visited frequently, when his wife was out or when she thought that he had gone to see his friends. They told him with many a happy laugh the joyful events of that day.

Obviously, Jacob was also very much surprised. "I have seen that poor child once in awhile in the street," he said. "I didn't know better than that her name was Mary and that she was a little niece of Madame Jordan. At least, that is what my wife told me. Incidentally, Madame Jordan is my wife's best friend, you know. Nobody in the city shows off as pious as Madame Jordan. Yet nobody in the whole neighborhood relishes gossip and slander more than she. She always knows the latest rumors and scandals and delights in talking about such things. Besides, it makes your blood boil when you see how she treats that unhappy child! She is always working and isn't allowed to play a single moment on the streets. The only time she is allowed outside is when she has to carry the parcels for the maidservant, who is as bad as her mistress. She is by far too haughty and too pious to talk to common people, but her face changes completely when she sees the very shadow of a priest. Then there is nobody as friendly, oily, and humble as she. No, she and her mistress are wicked women!"

After having discussed this new development for a long time, they decided at last that the next morning John and Camille would snoop around the house to find a way to help Manette escape. Jacob didn't know any better plan, but insisted that their chances to help Manette were very slim, indeed.

"The best thing is to go early," he said, "then Madame Jordan and her maid go to church and Manette has to stay home. Be careful now! In the meantime, I will try to find out more from my wife. You never know what information she may give. But one thing, boys: Whatever happens, mind you never admit that you know me! It is getting more and more dangerous and if you are caught, I want to stay out of the hands of the priests. Tomorrow night I'll try again to visit you for I'm curious to see how you will manage."

As soon as Manette entered the house that day, a tempest broke loose. Juliette, the maid, grasped her arm and pulled her to the living room where Madame Jordan was reading a prayer book. In the hallway the maid had scolded Manette at the top of her voice, but now she told with much excitement that Mary had talked with a boy who obviously knew her. She had heard herself that he called her Manette, and nobody in all of Paris knew that she had another name than Mary!

Hearing this, Madame also became angry, and both women began to slap and pinch Manette in the hope of forcing the boy's name out of her. It didn't help that the poor girl insisted never having seen the boy. They didn't believe her and tried hard to get her to admit he was her brother. When they didn't succeed, they sent her to bed, or rather, to the corner of the attic where she was supposed to sleep.

In the meantime, both women talked about that "wicked" child. At last, after they had gone over everything they knew about Manette, Madame Jordan went to a drawer, opened it and took a letter from it. She showed it to Juliette and said, "It is good that the Reverend Father Francis wrote about her brother's escape. I haven't shown this letter to anybody, not even to our own Reverend Father, who is also obligated to take care of Manette. I never expected her brother to find her. Now things have changed and you must go to the priest so that he can read this letter. Maybe he has some idea how to catch the boy. If they put a watch at the city gates, he cannot leave without falling into their hands. As far as the girl is concerned, leave her alone until tomorrow. Then we will see what the Reverend Father suggests we do."

Juliette rushed with the letter to the priest and returned rather soon with the message that he was thankful for the letter, but that they shouldn't worry for he would send two servants as soon as they saw the boy again. He didn't think it necessary to warn the magistrates. As long as Manette was kept in the house the boy wouldn't leave Paris for he had undoubtedly planned to take her with him.

Happy for the compliment from the reverend priest and glad that he took care of the matter, the women talked for hours about the blessings of the Roman Church, the friendliness of the priest and the wickedness of all heretics, especially the Huguenots.

14

MANETTE'S LIBERATION

John and Camille kept a close watch on the house the following morning. Standing together would have drawn too much attention from casual pedestrians. So they stood a fair distance away from each other. Their positions had the additional advantage that they could keep an eye on the house from both sides.

Nothing happened for a long time. However, they didn't know that Juliette had seen Camille through the window. She called her mistress, who was also very anxious to see the boy who was so interested in Manette. After a quick glance she fully agreed with Juliette that it certainly must be Manette's brother.

"Watch his face!" she whispered. "It's even more wicked-looking than his sister's!"

"One can never trust such trash," Juliette replied in a low voice. "No doubt, he would gladly kill us if he had a chance."

Both whispered although it wasn't necessary, but in their excitement they forgot that Camille couldn't hear them! After watching him a long time they became bored because nothing happened and so they went back to their work.

Later Madame Jordan happened to look out the window again and saw that Camille was still standing across the street. It gave her an unpleasant feeling. Did he expect that hussy to go outside or was he waiting for an opportunity to talk to her through the window?

Wait, she knew how to get rid of him! She quickly called Juliette, who grabbed a basket and went outside as if she were going to the market. However, after she had turned the street corner, so that Camille didn't see her changing directions, she went straight to the priest and told him that Manette's brother was watching Madame Jordan's house. The priest had quite a time trying to understand what she meant for she was so confusing that he got the impression that Manette had run away with her brother. At last, after letting her repeat the story, he understood that Manette was still in the house and that her brother was standing outside in the street.

"Are you sure that he is her brother?"

"Of course, he looks exactly like her." she said.

"This is no matter for the magistrate," he pondered. "It is better if we can keep it in our own hands. Maybe we can lock him up for a few hours. I don't have time now, but tonight I can interrogate him and see if he is indeed her brother. We can ask his village priest if he wants the boy returned or whatever. He should at least pay us well for all the trouble the boy is giving us." After some more thinking the priest soon devised a mean scheme for catching the boy.

John had watched and studied the house also for several hours. After a woman — it must be the maidservant, he thought — had left the house nothing happened. He had hoped that both women would have gone to church for then they might have had a chance to do something. Naturally, the door would be locked but he might try throwing small pebbles against the windows until Manette would hear him. When she saw him, she would open the door and they would run away. If she did not hear him, he would at least be able to figure out how to get into the house himself. In such a house there must be some window he could use for climbing inside. True, all the windows seemed to be closed, but one of them must have been forgotten. He was too far away to see clearly, but one appeared to be just a little ajar. It was too small for a man to go through but a boy like himself might just make it.

He became more and more impatient. How long would it take for the other woman to leave the house? Jacob had assured them that they went to Mass every morning, but today they surely didn't!

He looked down the street where Camille was standing and wondered if he was also growing impatient. He saw that Camille hadn't moved much. He was still in the same spot where he had seen him during the last half hour or so. After a few moments he turned his eyes away from Camille and lazily scanned the few people that walked in the street until he suddenly tensed up. What was happening now? Where did she come from? Behind Camille's back, he saw the woman who had left the house earlier. A heavily built man walked beside her.

All at once he realized the danger. His first impulse was to yell to Camille, but he changed his mind when he saw that it wouldn't help. Both went to Camille, and the woman seemed to say something. Camille, turning his head to the noise behind him, ducked impulsively and tried to run, but couldn't make it. The man grasped his collar and pulled him back with one hand and with his other hand he took hold of the boy's arm and then walked away pulling Camille with him. All of Camille's struggling was in vain. He couldn't loosen the man's hold, and was partially dragged, partially forced to walk. The woman said goodbye to the man, crossed the street and went inside the house again.

When John saw the woman entering the house he understood what had happened. Obviously, she must have seen Camille, had grown suspicious and had warned somebody to catch him. Panic-stricken he saw them go down the street. This would be the end of their journey together, he thought. Yet, he couldn't give up that easily. Maybe all was not lost, although the situation was very grim! Nobody knew that Camille wasn't a Romanist and they might only interrogate him for his roaming along the streets. Camille was smart enough not to betray himself and after all, he had seen Manette only once in his life. It was puzzling, though, that Camille wasn't caught by the sheriff or soldiers. The man looked just like a common laborer. What could be the reason, he wondered. Well, the only thing at the moment was to follow them and to find out where they were going. For a moment he considered helping Camille by jumping on the man's back, but then he realized how foolish it would be to do such a thing. The man was so strongly built that he could easily keep Camille and himself under control. Besides, there were always people around and they might be willing to help the man or might ask questions he didn't care to answer.

He didn't have to follow them far. After they went down a few streets they came to a large building, which John recognized as a monastery. Still holding Camille, the man walked to the large doors and knocked.

Presently, the door opened and both were admitted. A few minutes later the door opened again, the man reappeared and went away without looking around.

Now John realized that everything was really lost! Camille, locked up in a cloister, which could only mean that they knew who he was!

He waited for more than an hour hoping that Camille might appear again but nothing happened. Camille was inside and remained inside! It was a terrible situation and he didn't know what he could do to help him. Maybe Jacob could, but deep in his heart he knew that Jacob would never risk it. It was far too dangerous! Humanly speaking, nothing could be done. Yet, wasn't everything possible with God? A wordless prayer came from his heart while he slowly trudged back to their sleeping place. Even his chances to help Manette were gone, he thought. Obviously, that woman must have become suspicious and would now guard Manette even closer than ever!

Suddenly it crossed his mind that the city wasn't only dangerous for Camille, but also for him! Many people knew that they belonged together, and who knows, perhaps they were already looking for him, too. The next few days he had to stay in hiding until it was safe again. Well, he could stay in the stable as long as Jacob would bring him food. He trusted Jacob was willing to help for a considerable length of time.

Dishearted, John slowly shuffled back to the stable. He was less than a block away when he suddenly stopped. Two women were walking in front of him. One he recognized instantly, the maid who had helped catch Camille. The other one was her mistress. This woman treats Manette as a kind of slave, he thought bitterly.

When they were close to *In The Fishing Cat* they crossed the street, opened the door of the inn and went inside. At first he was only thankful that they hadn't seen him, but suddenly he realized that this was precisely what he had waited for the whole, long day. Nobody was in the house but Manette! Now he had his chance to get her out! Climbing through the window can be dangerous because any passer-by may see me, he thought, but it is worth the risk. If he succeeded, Manette would be free!

It was already getting dark and few people were on the street at that time of day. If he was careful, nobody would be able to see him climb into the house. Involuntarily, he began to run toward the house while making his plans, but slowed down at the end of the street. It was better not to draw attention by hurrying along so much.

He made himself walk with a brisk step and very soon he reached the house. The small window was still ajar. It was rather easy for a healthy boy like John to go through it. Just as he had expected, it was the kitchen window. Once inside, he glanced around and listened. Not seeing or hearing anything, he opened the door and went into a small hallway where he saw a few other doors.

After a moment's hesitation, he opened one of them at random, which appeared to lead into the living room. Nobody there! Quickly he tried the other two doors, which both led to small bedrooms. She wasn't there either and all at once he became scared, not seeing her. Suppose that she had been taken away! Anything was possible with those women! Nervously he began to call Manette's name hoping that she would hear him and call back. Being in a stranger's house where he wasn't allowed, he didn't dare to call too loud, afraid somebody in the street might hear him. Where could she be if not in these rooms? He looked for a basement but couldn't find a basement entrance. He didn't see a door to the attic either. If she was there, she must have heard him by now, he thought. In his desperation, he called again, this time somewhat louder, but he didn't get an answer. After a few moments, though, he heard a very soft sound, as if somebody was sobbing. Frantic, he searched all the rooms again, but was unable to discover where the sound came from. Maybe it wasn't Manette at all, he thought. Again he called, "If you are here somewhere, Manette, tell me where you are!"

This time he heard a muffled reply, "Yes, I am here in the attic."

Suddenly he remembered that he hadn't searched the kitchen very well. He went back. Oh, yes, in the small kitchen was another door that he had overlooked when he had entered the house. He opened it and saw a narrow, steep staircase.

He raced upstairs, skipping two and three steps at a time. The attic was so low that he had to stoop, not wanting to hit his head. Across the attic was a door with a small latch. With three large steps he reached it, lifted the latch, opened the door, and the next moment he had a little, crying girl in his arms. He himself was also very much moved while he patted her encouragingly on her shoulder. He couldn't say anything, and Manette couldn't stop crying, although she sometimes laughed through her tears while hugging John. After awhile, they calmed down somewhat and began to talk excitedly. Later, John could never remember what they had said, and how long they had held each other. It must have been a long time! At last, John pulled himself together, loosened Manette's arms and said, "We must leave immediately! Hurry! Take all your things and let's go before those women come back. Later we can talk as much as we want, but now we must hurry!"

"Yes, let's go! I can't take anything for I have nothing. Come!" Manette pushed him toward the stairs afraid that they had waited too long. However, it was already too late!

At the very same moment as they came to the stairs, the street door opened, and they heard both women entering. Manette who was ahead of John stopped, not knowing what to do. John, more used to unexpected situations, grasped her arm and pulled her back into the room. He closed the door when they were inside so that the latch at the outside of the door, fell into its lock. Manette heard it and could barely suppress a cry of terror.

"John, we can't get out anymore. We are locked in this room," she whispered.

John, knowing how simple it was to open the lock with his knife, laughed silently and whispered in her ear, "Don't worry, honey! I can open the door any time with my knife."

He looked around the little room, but it was too dark to see much. He saw on the floor in a corner of the room some old rags. With his mouth close to her ears, he asked if that was her bed and when she nodded, he told her that he was going to lie down between the bed and the wall. She must cover him up with the rags so that nobody could see him and then lie down as well and pretend to be sleeping. It was, after all, entirely possible that these women would come to make sure that she was still there! Manette didn't think so for she couldn't remember anybody ever coming to the attic, as long as she had been staying with Madame Jordan.

It was good that she had obeyed him, anyway. Juliette had found the door to the attic open, and she and her mistress were wondering if the door had blown open, or if Manette had managed to get downstairs.

"It would really not be difficult for her to break the lock to her room and run away," said Madame Jordan and she sent Juliette upstairs with a candle to investigate the matter. She herself didn't dare to go. She was scared of mice and thought there must be lots of them in the attic. Juliette, grumbling about the whims of her mistress and the troubles Manette gave them, climbed upstairs, opened the attic door and looked inside. Fortunately, she didn't walk into the room, but when she saw Manette asleep in the corner, she felt that the door must have blown open. Without saying anything, she went downstairs again and told Madame Jordan that the wicked child was sleeping as if she would never wake up anymore.

A few hours later, both women were asleep while Manette and John waited in the attic until it was safe for them to leave. This gave John enough time to think matters over and had decided to get out that very same night. Tomorrow morning when the women would go to church it would probably be easier to leave, but it might be too late. It was risky and dangerous to slip silently through the house while the occupants were home, but it must be done! If he was found in this house he knew what would happen — he would spend the rest of his life in jail and life would even be more unbearable for Manette in a nunnery, where she would be sent. He must go and Manette must go with him. He wouldn't dare leave her behind, not even for a few hours!

"Come on, Manette," he whispered after it had been quiet downstairs for a long time. "Let's get going! Be careful for they must not hear us." Silently they stood up and tiptoed to the door.

15

BROTHER BENEDICT, THE FOOLISH JAILER

It was embarrassing and humiliating for Camille to be caught in the street unexpectedly, but he had only himself to blame. After watching the house for a few hours with nothing happening, he had become somewhat careless and hadn't given proper attention to the people passing by or even to the house itself, for that matter. He had been daydreaming about his parents. Suddenly he had heard somebody talking behind his back. It was a woman's voice saying, "That's him, Mary's brother!" He turned, understood the situation and tried to run. At that moment a man grasped him and shook him vehemently. Camille struggled and wrestled, but couldn't wriggle himself loose and very soon had to give up for the man pinched his neck as if he would rather strangle him than let him run away. When Camille quieted down a moment to get his breath, his attacker shifted his grip quickly. One hand held his arm like a vise, the other one clamped his neck tightly, and so he was forced to walk along without being able to resist anymore. Other people in the street saw the man grabbing him, but nobody showed enough interest to interfere or even ask what was going on. The man took Camille to a monastery a few blocks away where he knocked at the gate.

A sheepish-looking monk opened the door and seemed rather surprised to see the unexpected visitors. The man didn't waste any words in explaining his visit. He pushed Camille inside, took a letter out of his shirt and gave it to the monk, without releasing Camille's neck.

"This letter is for the abbot. In it, Father Ambrose requests that this boy be held for a few hours until he can find some time to interrogate him."

The monk's face dropped as he replied, "You'd better come back tonight for the abbot is not in. He will be rather late in returning."

The man made a wry face and said, "You don't think I will hold on to this boy all day, do you? He is a dangerous Huguenot. We have no place to lock him up ourselves, so I brought him here. You monks have ample opportunities to put this boy safely away and you'd better do it."

"Holy Mary," the monk suddenly shouted, frightened. "Is that boy a heretic? I never saw such a young one in all my life. How can a good-looking boy like him be so wicked? Sometimes Satan hides himself in the garb of a saint, though, and that must be the case here. But where can I keep him? I have to stay at the door and I don't know if we have a cell strong enough to secure him! No, we can't keep him. Why don't you try some other place?"

The man became impatient. "Now you listen to me!" he said. "The abbot will certainly give you a hard time if you let this good catch slip through your fingers. Tonight he will be interrogated, and then Father Ambrose will take him back again."

"Oh, yes, but don't you think that he might escape, anyway? I have been told that Huguenots have made a pact with the devil. Maybe the devil will help him to sneak out!"

Throughout the whole conversation, the monk had been crossing himself. Truly, he was a simple soul and very superstitious. He was genuinely scared that the devil would help Camille and that no cell could keep him.

The man had quite a time persuading the monk that Camille was just a common Huguenot boy who surely would never get any help from Hell. At last the monk gave in and opened the door of a small cell, just a few yards away from the main entrance.

"He can never get out of here if it's true what you say. You are sure that he isn't dangerous, are you?"

The man didn't even take the trouble of replying, but looked into the cell. When he saw that it was well-suited for its purpose, he pushed Camille roughly inside, locked the door and returned the key to the monk.

"If I were you, I would check the boy every once in a while," he warned. "Nothing could be worse for you than if your abbot or Father Ambrose does not find him here tonight."

Without wasting more words, he went to the door and disappeared before the monk could say anything.

Camille fell to the ground from the man's hard push. Slowly he scrambled up, rubbing his neck and looked around. The cell was apparently used regularly by a monk, and was rather bare. In one corner was a crib with a straw mattress. Next to it stood a prayer chair and on the wall hung an image of Mary with the Christ child in her arms. One of the walls had a window, but it was rather high, and far too small to use to escape. The door was made of oak, very massive and obviously locked.

Downhearted he sat down on the mattress. He was in a desperate pinch. If he couldn't escape soon John might be caught also. He knew that his chances to breakout were nearly nonexistent, though. The one tiny ray of hope was that they thought that he was John. Who knows, they might let him go when they discovered their mistake. Yet, it was most unlikely. How could they find out their error without knowing either John or him? And when they began interrogating him, it was easy enough for them to determine that he was also a Huguenot! What would they do when they realized that? Would he have to spend the rest of his life in a little cell in a cloister? Just thinking about it made him shake with fear!

Everything had gone wrong. He was caught and very soon John might also fall into their hands. In a sudden impulse he fell on his knees and began to pray. He couldn't think of good-sounding words, but asked, faltering, for strength and courage so that he wouldn't deny his Savior.

After his prayer he felt calm. He stood up and seated himself again on the mattress. It was unlikely that anything would happen soon for it was still early in the afternoon and the exchange of words between the monk and the man had made it clear that he wouldn't be disturbed before nightfall.

Brother Benedict, whose duty it was to open the gate for visitors, was not only a simple soul, but also had an inveterate thirst for rumors. Any kind of scandal or gossip was welcome to him for he used it, embellished with his own imaginations, for slanderous attacks on innocent people. Sometimes it led him into trouble, but nothing could cure him of the ugly desire to poke his nose into other people's business.

Gradually he got used to the idea that a Huguenot boy was occupying a cell in the cloister and he even began to enjoy the thought, although he remained somewhat afraid. He had never bothered to figure out what Huguenots were and what they stood for, but that didn't matter. They didn't pray to Mary and that alone was enough proof that they must be heretics. It came as a great surprise that it was only a boy and a very good-looking one at that. He had always thought that Huguenot boys didn't look like Roman Catholic boys, but more like criminals. Being the jailer of a Huguenot boy was a very important experience in his dull life and he intended to get the most out of it.

Every hour or so he shuffled to the cell and looked in at the boy. He didn't open the door to see him for it had a small wicket, made for keeping an eye on monks who might fall asleep during their long prayers. He had always hated that spy-hole, but today it was a good thing to have for now he could see everything in the cell without himself being seen.

Every time he took a look, he saw the boy sitting quietly on the mattress instead of being raging mad as he had secretly hoped. He was most disappointed.

Camille had been sitting on the bed several hours. He had enough sense to understand that it was useless to make a lot of noise. Nobody would bother to look even if they heard him, which he doubted for he hadn't heard anyone during all these hours. After the door had closed behind him, he had first considered his own situation, but afterward his thoughts had turned to John and Manette because he didn't see any way of escape for himself.

A few times he wondered if it wouldn't be advisable to talk a little with the monk, his jailer, and try to persuade him to let him go. He didn't try it for the simple reason that he doubted it would work. The monk would probably be far too scared of the abbot.

The only way to escape from the cell was through the door, which was locked. If the monk entered his cell he might try a sudden rush to the outside door, but the monk never opened the door and only peeked through the hole in it.

While looking at the door, he observed that its frame had a peculiar construction. A heavy board, nearly a foot wide and several feet long, was protruding above the door. It was clearly made to support the statue of a saint which had been removed later. Indifferently, he wondered how heavy a statue the board had supported, but gradually he became more animated for a plan of escape began to form in his mind. He waited until the monk had looked through the spy hole again, and as soon as the sound of the annoying footsteps indicated that the monk had gone, Camille became very busy.

Taking the mattress, he propped it up against the wall underneath the window, which made the impression that he had used the contraption to climb out! Next he went to the door and, after several attempts, succeeded in climbing up on the protruding board. It was very difficult because he had to do it without making any noise that would alert Brother Benedict. Happily, the door posts were carved with ornaments, which he used as support for his toes.

The exercise took less time than he had expected and with a sigh of relief he laid himself quietly down on the board.

The next half hour nothing happened except that he became more and more uncomfortable for he didn't dare to move, fearing he would fall off. He was just beginning to wonder, how much longer he could hold his cramped position when he heard the monk shuffling to the wicket again. He anxiously waited for the monk to react. The next minute would show if his plan would be a success or a failure.

Brother Benedict was bored. Not a single visitor had knocked on the gate the last few hours and most of this time he had been sitting on his chair in the hall fighting against sleep. Well, he'd better go and see what the boy was doing. It would be fun to have a chat with him and find out where he came from and how he had been caught. It would probably be an interesting story to tell during suppertime!

He opened the wicket and looked inside, expecting to see the boy still sitting on the mattress as he had done all afternoon. But the boy had disappeared! Rubbing his eyes furiously, he wondered if he was dreaming or if it had to do with witchcraft. Where could he be? Had he escaped in spite of the locked door? Look, the mattress was standing against the wall underneath the window! Had he used it for climbing through it?

He generally wasn't a man of quick action, but now he took the key out of his pocket in a sudden impulse, opened the door and rushed to the window to see if he could see the boy in the garden. He tried to climb the mattress without realizing that the window with its iron bars was by far too small for a boy to creep through. The mattress, which could not bear his heavy weight collapsed, and the monk fell on the floor. Quickly, he jumped up and hurried out of the cell without taking the time to close the door. The window opened into the garden and it was always possible that the boy couldn't climb the high garden wall. Maybe he could get hold of him before he managed to scale it. He ran through the corridor, opened a small side door and disappeared into the garden for a thorough search.

Camille, lying on his high board, had seen everything. It was very difficult not to laugh aloud, especially when the monk rolled off the mattress and raced away. This part of his plan had worked wonderfully!

Climbing down in a hurry made his foot slip and he crashed down to the floor. In his excitement he felt no pain, scrambled up again, leaped into the empty corridor and ran to the main entrance. He turned the knob, but the door didn't open. All at once he became frightened. Was the door locked? Again he turned the knob while pulling with all his strength but to no avail. Desperate, he tried over and over again until his hands began to ache, but without the desired result. Suddenly he saw the key sticking in the lock, and just in time, for he heard somewhere a door opening and footsteps.

Turning the key was a matter of seconds and then it was easy to push the door open. Brother Benedict, returning discouraged from the garden, came in time to see Camille opening the door. He made a sudden dash in an effort to grab him, but fortunately failed.

Camille ran outside to freedom, but just when he jumped down the steps, two monks were climbing up. One of them, who realized that something must be wrong when a boy comes dashing out of a monastery, stretched out his arm to catch the boy, but Camille managed to avoid him by ducking unexpectedly. He couldn't slow down in time and ran so hard against the other monk's legs that they both went sprawling on the ground.

Brother Benedict, who had run after the boy, stumbled also and all of them formed a screaming heap of moving legs and arms. Camille, being young and therefore the fastest, was the first one on his feet and without a moment's delay, continued running. He kept going until he was far away from the cloister but then he had to slacken his pace due to a pain in his side.

The stress caused by the events of the last hours was over, and now he felt all done in. Yet, he had to keep moving as fast as possible and remain on guard all the time so he would not fall into their hands again. Feverishly his brain worked. He couldn't walk the streets too long, but must go into hiding as soon as possible without anybody noticing. The only safe place was the stable, but he had no choice. He couldn't wait for the evening! The streets were far too dangerous!

He was amazed that he was so calm and could figure out what to do and which precautions to take in such a dangerous situation without losing his alertness for safety. Frequently he looked back to make sure that nobody followed him and he also took the trouble to peep around the street corners whenever needed. The last street before turning into the lane leading to the stable, was a very quiet street, so that he could take his time. He waited until the whole street was empty before slipping through the alley into the stable. With a heavy sigh of satisfaction he closed the door and went upstairs.

The stable was empty, of course. Most likely John had taken to his heels and if not, he might even be watching the house yet. He would probably come home after dark, anyway.

After eating some bread, Camille fell down on his straw mattress and was soon asleep, utterly exhausted from all the adventures of that day. Late in evening he awoke and was surprised to see that John hadn't arrived yet. Could they have caught him, too? He decided to stay awake until John came home, but that could take a very long time. He waited and waited without hearing John's steps. Listening to all the noises of the city and the stable, he became worried about John's safety. At last he couldn't stand it anymore and went downstairs to listen at the outside door. He did not hear anything. Most people had gone to bed and it was quiet in the street. Again, he went upstairs, not knowing what to do, and went to bed, trying hard to keep himself under control. Around midnight he fell into a troubled sleep again without knowing it. He was plagued with terrible dreams and nightmares about John and himself being jailed and tortured. A few hours later he suddenly woke up because he thought he heard footsteps on the stairs. He raised himself on his elbow to listen better. Yet, he heard steps, indeed. Somebody was coming to the attic. No, not one but two persons were climbing the stairs, no doubt about it. Who could they be? he wondered, becoming frightened. Not John, for he would be alone. Was the hiding place discovered and had they waited for the night to catch him again?

Terrified, he listened to the sound of the footsteps coming closer and closer and he heard somebody say in a low voice, "Be careful now, Manette. This is the end of the stairs."

But he knew that voice! It was John's. The other one must be Manette! John must have freed her and brought her to the hiding place. Delighted, he jumped up and hurried to John, who had just entered the attic.

John, who thought that Camille was still in the monastery, gave the poor boy such a push that he fell head over heels back on his mattress. At the same time he recognized Camille's voice from his cry of pain when he was pushed over. He stepped forward, grasped Camille's shoulder, and pulled him up onto his legs so that he could see Camille's face. When he saw that it was really Camille, he gave him a heavy slap on his shoulder out of sheer joy, which Camille returned. Within a few seconds they were struggling and wrestling with each other like a pair of young puppies.

Manette had waited quietly without understanding what was going on. She became frightened seeing the rough dealing between the boys and began to sob softly. She thought that Camille had hidden himself and intended to bring John to the sheriff. As soon as John heard her, he stopped and said, "Manette, this is Camille of whom I've told you. He is the best friend I ever had and if he hadn't seen you at the market, I would never have found you."

Through her tears she looked at Camille, but couldn't distinguish his face in the darkness. When he said a few words of welcome, she relaxed for she recognized his voice easily.

They talked for hours about the many things that had happened that day. John told how the adventurous night in the attic of Madame Jordan's house had ended. Around midnight he had carefully removed the lock of the attic door with his knife without waking up the women downstairs. They had quietly sneaked downstairs and without making any noise, had left the house through the front door, which could be opened from the inside. Then, they had gone to the stable, where to their happy surprise, they had found Camille.

Camille, of course, also told how he had escaped from the cloister and John couldn't understand how Camille ever had the bright idea of hiding himself above the door. They kept on talking and repeating themselves for a good many hours until Manette was so terrible tired that they decided to go to sleep for a few hours.

16

CAMILLE CHANGES INTO A GIRL

It was early morning. Jacob had opened his inn at the usual hour and was busy cleaning up. He never did such work at night after closing hours, but always in the morning because he had more light and, as a rule, there were no customers.

Having swept the floor, he had wiped the tables and chairs with a damp cloth, and was now rinsing all the glasses in a large, water-filled dish-pan. Just when he began to take the beautiful clean glasses out of the pan for drying, the door was thrown open and somebody hurried in. It was Juliette!

"Where is your wife, Jacob?" she asked, but without waiting for an answer she opened the door and disappeared into the living room. Dumbfounded, Jacob looked at the already closed door.

"Isn't she in a hurry?" he pondered while he continued his work. "I wonder what has happened."

A few moments later the living room door opened again and his wife appeared.

"Jacob, you must go to Madame Jordan. Her little niece has run away."

Jacob was startled, but managed to hide his surprise. He pretended to be annoyed with this interruption in his work.

"Nobody ever told me that Madame Jordan had her niece staying with me. If that girl has run away, well, I can't help it. It's her business, isn't it?"

"Don't be a boor, Jacob," his wife said. "Just come in for a few moments and listen to Juliette's story. Maybe you can tell us what to do. Madame Jordan is one of my best friends and you could at least show some interest in her difficulties!"

Seeing that his wife was quite determined, he slowly dried his hands and followed her to the living room, where an excited Juliette was waiting. She told him that in the morning they had discovered that Mary, the little niece, was gone. She always slept in the attic,

132

but the lock was cut out of the door and they hadn't been able to find her. They couldn't figure out how the girl could have left the house because every night Madame Jordan locked the outside door herself and kept the key in her bedroom.

"Maybe she is hiding in a closet," Jacob remarked without much interest. He didn't like the idea of locking that girl in her room at night, but was smart enough not to mention it.

"Yes," Juliette said, "We thought the same thing and have searched the whole house, without finding her. That is the reason why Madame sent me over to ask if Jacob would be kind enough to help find her. Maybe you can discover how she was able to leave the house for we haven't the faintest idea. We didn't hear anything last night and her brother couldn't have helped her either since he was caught early in the morning!"

Hearing this, Jacob became really alarmed. So John had been caught! Happily, he had himself so well under control that he didn't show any emotions that could betray him. Casually, as if he didn't know anything, he asked, "Her brother? Oh, she had more relatives, did she?"

That simple question was enough to start his wife and Juliette telling the story of Mary, which he, of course, already knew. He pretended to listen very attentively, but in the meantime worried about John.

"How did her brother ever come here, to Paris?" he asked.

"That boy, a staunch heretic, fled his village many months ago. Father Francis of Lisieux sent word that the boy could be on his way here. We didn't pay much attention to his letter for we thought it impossible for the boy to come so far without being caught. But the day before yesterday I saw him at the market! He was quietly sitting on the edge of the fountain with a pile of baskets and talked to Mary when I wasn't there to watch. Yesterday he stood outside our house! I quickly went to the priest to tell him and he sent somebody, who caught the boy and took him to the cloister of the Benedictines."

It was the first time that Jacob's wife heard Juliette mention the baskets and all at once she recalled that particular event of a few weeks ago.

"Jacob, don't you remember the basket-makers you threw out on the street because they couldn't pay? Don't you think this boy may be one of the two? There must be two boys rather than only one."

"Oh, I don't think so," Jacob said. "Of course, it is always possible, but very unlikely. It happened too long ago."

Deep in his heart, he was very glad that he had been smart enough to make the impression of chasing them away. Now it would be difficult to prove that he had helped them! Yet, it would be good to talk with Madame Jordan for she might tell him something that he could use for his own safety!

During his short walk towards Madame Jordan's house, he decided that he had had enough of the whole situation. It was becoming too dangerous! One of these days they would find out his part in the adventure. Maybe he was already under suspicion because John may have said too much. He had helped the boys because he knew that his old mother would be pleased if she knew. But he had to stop. He could only go so far, and that was more than other people did. Enough is enough. After all, he had already taken a very large risk because he couldn't do anything to prevent John mentioning his name. If that had happened, it would already be too late. But wait, he thought, the first step in the proper direction would be for him to betray Camille and Manette to the police. In that case he would surely be on good terms with the priests! He could always claim that he had given the boys food and shelter for so many weeks to understand their plans and catch them red-handed when they tried to kidnap Manette! However, he knew that he couldn't do such a mean thing to them. For the time being he would just take his chances and do nothing, he decided. Hopefully everything would turn out for the best, anyway!

Obviously, his search of the house didn't reveal anything of importance. It was rather easy for him to understand how Manette had disappeared while the outside door was locked because he found the little kitchen window ajar. Out of precaution, he didn't say anything about it, but as soon as he had an opportunity, he closed the small window without the women noticing it. It was a pleasant surprise to find how well the boys had managed, although, John was jailed, that was bad. He frowned deep in thought.

An hour later, Jacob considered again his situation while walking home. It wasn't as bad as he had initially thought. Nobody knew of his involvement with the boys, and if it came out, so what? He could only be accused of giving a sleeping place to some homeless children. The excellent reputation of his inn and the large number of monks and nuns who loved drinking his wine would make a joke of any court trial. The most he would get would be a fine, if anything!

He was delighted that Manette had escaped. After seeing the small attic room where she had slept, he had been thoroughly shocked. The room wasn't even good for a pigsty and much less for a human being. He wasn't sure where she was now, but Camille, being a smart boy, probably had taken her into hiding in the stable. He was sorry that John was caught, but boys of his age usually were sent to a monastery rather than the galleys. Maybe he would find another opportunity to run away in the future, who knows? Yes, everything considered, the situation was not bad at all!

His wife was talking with the few early-morning customers about Mary's running away when he entered. She was annoyed that she had to serve them because her husband was needed at Madame Jordan's house.

"Couldn't you have hurried? You surely took your time, didn't you? Did you find the girl? Where is she now?"

"Well, you didn't expect her to stay in the house after having escaped from her attic room, did you? I don't know how she could have left the house if not through the door. Madame Jordan remembered to have locked the door last night, but wasn't sure if it was unlocked this morning. She isn't very smart, I think, for it took me nearly half an hour of questioning before she admitted that the key was always left in the lock on the inside so that it was easy for the girl to open the door."

"Rather foolish of Madame Jordan," his wife commented candidly. "It doesn't make that much difference, though. It's a matter of a few hours before the girl will be picked up again. She is most likely just walking the streets because she will hardly have the guts to go through the city gates in daytime without her brother.

"She has no guts?" Jacob asked, amazed. "How wrong you are! A girl who cuts the lock out of her bedroom door and sneaks past the bedroom of her mistress, is smart and brave. She must have left the city as soon as the gates were opened, I bet."

The real surprise came a few hours later. This time, Madame Jordan and Juliette both came and told the exciting story that Mary's brother had escaped from the monastery after a terrible fight. The rather innocent stumbling on the stairs had been exaggerated into a terrible fight because everybody who told the story had added something to it. Madame had heard the story from the priest himself whom she had visited to tell him that Mary had run away. Undoubtedly, both disappearances must be related as Madame Jordan had thought from the very beginning.

A heavy weight was lifted from Jacob's heart now that everything had turned out so well. Of course, he acted as if he couldn't care less, yet deep in his heart he was glad that all three children were free again. They must be in the stable and he made up his mind that he would visit them at night. He wasn't under any suspicion for the boys must have kept their mouths shut! After all, they were two splendid fellows! Everything would be superb if he only could get them safely out of Paris.

In the meantime, John, Camille, and Manette were sitting quietly in the hay above the stable. The day passed quickly because they had a lot to tell each other. Manette's story, especially, made a deep impression on the boys, who were furious and shook their fists while listening.

After she had been taken away from her home, she had stayed almost a week in Father Francis' house before she was sent to Paris. Then John understood that she hadn't been away when Father Francis had told Mother that she was gone. He became angrier still when he heard how the women had treated her. They had wanted her to pray to Mary, and when she didn't do it she was beaten. When that didn't help, they had tied her down to the grating of the fireplace and threatened to burn her alive if she didn't pray to Mary. She must have fainted for she remembered only that she awoke in that horrible attic room.[16] From that time on she was forced to go to church every morning and was spanked when she came home. The rest of the day she had to help in the kitchen and go to the market with Juliette. She wasn't allowed to eat with them and got only the left overs. It wasn't much, for the women cooked just enough for themselves. She wasn't allowed to talk with anyone either, and when the women went away, she was locked in her room.

John admired his brave little sister and comforted her as well as possible. Now he would take care of her, he told her, and she didn't

---

[16] A girl of seven years old was treated like Manette in the city of Louden in 1681.

need to be scared anymore. As soon as they had left Paris, she would find out how much fun it was to walk along the country roads to Holland and they certainly would be there in a few weeks.

Jacob, who hadn't known that there were now three in the stable had given them the usual amount of food. This was not enough, especially since Manette was very hungry, never having been allowed to eat her fill. Without saying anything, John and Camille winked at each other and purposely ate very slowly and very little so that Manette could eat as much as she wanted.

At night they discussed possible ways of leaving Paris. They expected the city gates to be watched during the next few days and therefore felt it best to stay in the stable where it was safe and comfortable. True, it wouldn't be dangerous for John because nobody knew him, but it was far different for Manette and Camille. However, for the moment they didn't worry about it. They had enough time to look into this problem tomorrow or even the day after!

Late at night they heard the well known steps of Jacob on the stairs and were glad to see him. He was rather late because it had taken some time to find a good excuse to leave the house.

He listened openmouthed when they told him the true story of their escape and roared with laughter upon hearing how Camille had bumped into the monks and that all of them had rolled down the stairs.

"Oh, boy, I wish I had seen you bouncing on those monks," he said, rubbing his tears of laughter away.

At the end of his visit he advised them to leave as soon as possible for it was dangerous to stay much longer for both himself and the children. Besides, it was getting late in the year and they must try hard to be in Holland before freezing weather began.

All three of them agreed. They admitted, though, that they didn't have the faintest idea of how to leave Paris without running the risk of being caught again. Jacob didn't expect the city gates to be watched. So many people lived in Paris that nobody would be interested in three children who had run away, even if they were Huguenot children. Obviously, they must ensure that the few people who had seen them wouldn't recognize them. You never knew!

"Don't you worry," he added. "I have thought about it the whole afternoon and I think I know what you should do. Mind, anyone who wants to catch you is looking for a boy of about fourteen and a girl of ten or eleven. Nobody will suspect a fourteen-year-old country-girl and her little ten-year-old brother to be runaways, right?"

Baffled by his mystifying words, they looked at him inquisitively. What could he mean?

"I always thought you were smart and yet you don't understand me?" Jacob said, laughing. "It is as simple as possible. We'll dress Camille to look like a girl and change Manette into a nice boy. It's easy enough! I don't think I'll have any trouble picking up some clothes and you have enough time to alter them if they don't fit well enough."

"Yes, but what about their hair?" John asked. "It's easy enough to cut off Manette's hair, but we can't grow it on Camille's head."

Jacob laughed even harder.

"That is what you think! But how wrong you are. It is very easy to grow hair, not on Camille's head, but on his cap. We'll sew Manette's hair to a bonnet and as long as he keeps it on his head, nobody will suspect anything."

All three had to laugh about it. Camille, dressed up as a girl with long hair — could anything be more ridiculous? But they agreed that it was an excellent idea!

Jacob now said goodbye to them for they felt it would be safer if he didn't come anymore. Tomorrow night he would place some clothes and sewing material next to the food. Next, he would give them two more days of food and then expected them to leave. Again, he emphasized that they should never tell anybody his name and how he had helped them! For the second time, he said goodbye and left the hiding place, leaving the three excited children behind. At last they would begin the final part of their trip to freedom!

17

MANETTE'S NEW COAT

It had been raining for two days. The roads were muddy and everybody avoided going outside as much as possible. Who wouldn't appreciate the dry comfort of a good home in this wet weather? It wasn't a very heavy rain, though, just a miserable drizzle that penetrated everything and chilled to the bone.

John, Camille, and Manette had walked for hours and were thoroughly wet. When the rain began, they had stayed dry underneath a forgotten haystack, but when it kept coming down, they hadn't had the patience to wait any longer. They had continued their journey. All three of them were in a hurry to be in Holland before the real frost made travel impossible.

John worried a lot about Manette, especially today. She did her utmost not to lag behind, but she looked sick and felt miserable. She had large blisters on her feet because she was not used to walking long distances. She complained that her stomach ached and that she felt hot one moment and shivered with cold the next. Camille and John took good care of her and helped her as much as possible to make the going easier. They walked on either side of her with their arms around her for support. For a short time they had taken turns carrying her on their backs, but had to give up because she was too heavy.

John looked at Camille and saw that he understood that something more must be done. It was of the utmost importance to find shelter, but where? They knew from experience that most farmers didn't mind if they slept a few nights in their haylofts. Yet, if Manette grew sicker the priest would be warned and that would be the very worst that could happen to them. No, to stop at a farm was too risky!

Wearily they trudged along, wet, tired, and worried. Everything seemed to have turned for the worse after it had begun so well.

When they had left Paris, the future looked bright and they had made fun of everything. Even the danger seemed exciting. But all that had changed!

After Manette's escape they had stayed in Paris three more days. During that time they had altered the clothing Jacob had given them. They cut Manette's hair and sewed it to Camille's bonnet. Even John had trouble recognizing Camille in a girl's dress, and Manette looked like a nice little boy. Although several baskets were unsold, John didn't dare to take them for fear of being recognized. He had packed the largest basket with their few belongings, after first dirtying its outside. It wouldn't do to draw attention by carrying a basket that looked brand new and so he made sure that the basket looked like an old, well-used one.

Late in the afternoon when the streets were rather empty, they had gone through the city gates. It was a frightening experience but fortunately, Jacob had been right! Nobody paid any attention to them because they looked like farmer's children returning home, a farmer's boy, his sister and their little brother.

Once outside the city, they had continued walking most of the night with only a few rest periods. It seemed that they felt less afraid and more courageous with every additional mile they put between themselves and the city.

Camille felt that walking with long skirts was rather troublesome and kept complaining all the way, first as a kind of joke but more seriously as the day wore on. It was, indeed, difficult to avoid stepping on the skirt seam with his long legs and he had stumbled several times before he had mastered this difficulty. Manette and John made fun of his awkward way of walking, especially when he tried to run. He never became annoyed, though, and laughed along with them. However, he protested vehemently when John told him to wear the girl's dress a few days longer. They were still close to the city, and it wasn't worth the risk of being discovered, he explained patiently. If he had so much trouble with the skirt he could use a piece of rope to hoist it up somewhat to make walking easier.

Camille was, of course, quite pleased when he put on his own clothing again after a few days. Manette didn't bother changing to her own dress for she liked being dressed as a boy. It was such a good feeling to take large steps like boys without a skirt fluttering around her legs.

It was a pity that Manette was so weak. The boys discovered rapidly that they couldn't go as far as when just the two of them had been together. They shortened their daily walking distances and rested more often. They also needed new baskets to sell for food, and as soon as they were a safe distance from Paris they stopped for several days to weave a few. The delay meant a serious loss of time on their journey, but it had improved Manette's condition immensely.

The country in this part of France was different from the other parts through which they had come. There were a good number of hills, and it seemed to have a denser population, for they passed by countless farms. They also felt that the people were different. They talked a kind of dialect that the children could hardly understand.

The boys took good care of Manette! They never left her alone, and when one of them was selling baskets, the other one stayed with her. They also gave her all the food she could eat and she already had begun to lose her hollow appearance.

Unfortunately, Manette's feet began to hurt a few days after leaving Paris. In a very short time her feet were covered with large blisters. It was a good thing that John hadn't listened when Camille insisted that they throw away his gown because of his intense dislike for it. Now the cloth came in handy for bandaging Manette's sore feet. It had helped a lot, but walking was still very painful.

A few days before the rainfall began, the temperature dropped suddenly. Manette, who was thinly dressed and not used to living outdoors, had apparently caught a cold. She began to cough and felt miserable. Everything had gotten far worse when it began raining and now it became more and more clear that Manette was too sick to keep going. The boys had the impression that she sometimes didn't even know what was happening!

At last John made up his mind that it was impossible to go on. They decided to stop at the first farm they saw in spite of the risk. At that very same moment it happened! Suddenly Manette stumbled and would have fallen if the boys hadn't held her so tightly. Her face turned deathly pale, and they saw that she had fainted. Frightened, John called her name, but she didn't react at all! Surprised that she had fainted, the boys laid her carefully at the side of the path in the grass and tried to bring her back to consciousness, but all their efforts were in vain. She didn't stir!

The drizzle continued to fall, and at last, in desperation, John said, "Camille, we can't wait any more! I'll remain with her, and you go look for help. If she has to lay in the rain on the wet grass much longer, she may die! Hurry on and try to find someone who can help, but come back as soon as possible."

He had barely finished talking when Camille took off running as fast as he could, determined to do his utmost in getting help.

Hurriedly, John turned around knelt beside Manette and tried to lay her in a more comfortable position. He was frightened, stricken with sorrow and didn't know what to do. In his confusion, he began rubbing her hands and her face and after a few moments, she opened her eyes and whispered, "Where am I? Why am I so wet?" All at once she tried to struggle up but John pushed her carefully down.

"Don't worry, Manette. You have fainted, but I am here and will take care of you. Camille went away looking for a comfortable, dry spot."

"Oh, John. I am so cold. Will I die?"

"Of course not, silly," John quickly assured her. "As soon as Camille gets back, we will take you to a warm place and in no time you will feel comfortable again. Don't you worry! Everything will be fine soon."

His words sounded very hopeful but he hardly expected Camille to find a good place. It might take a long time before he came back, and even then, it would be most unlikely that he had found any help!

It was nearly an hour later when, at last, Camille appeared again. He was running and wasn't even close when he called out that he had found something. He stopped where Manette was laying, panting so much that he could barely talk.

"I didn't find any house or farm, but about twenty minutes down this path is a large thicket. I wondered if we couldn't get enough fallen branches inside it to build a kind of shelter, but inside I found an old shanty, not far from the path. It's nearly falling apart, but it's reasonably dry, although the roof leaks at different places. Let's go there. At least it's far better than here!"

John nodded without saying anything. He tried to lift Manette and carry her in his arms but she was too heavy. Therefore, he held her shoulders and Camille took her legs, and in this manner they carried her to the shack.

That shanty was, indeed, a sad looking mass of old logs, and didn't seem to be used anymore. It was open at one side and was, in reality, no more than an old, decayed lean-to. The ground was dry except for a few puddles where the roof leaked severely. Carefully, they placed Manette on the driest spot and began to work diligently to make her as comfortable as possible for the time being.

A big fire was badly needed, not only for warming themselves but also for drying their clothing. Camille was stunned when John told him to gather a pile of dry branches. Where could he find dry wood after two days of continuous rain had soaked everything? But John knew what he was talking about! He looked around and went to the back of the shed where he tore away one of the rotting boards of the wall.

"This wood is dry enough on the inside to start a fire. We can keep it going with wet branches, but we must dry them first," he said.

While Camille hurriedly gathered branches outside in the rain, John took his knife and cut a pile of thin, dry splinters from the board. Next he lighted them, using his old tinderbox, which he carried in one of his pockets and within a few minutes he had a nice fire going. He had made the fire toward the open side of the shack so that the smoke would go outside and the heat would warm the inside. The wet branches that Camille had gathered were piled beside the fire to dry.

Half an hour later it began feeling comfortable inside the shed. John and Camille sat in front of the fire and discussed in whispers how to prepare a comfortable sleeping place for Manette. Obviously, without good material nothing could be done, so John finally said that he would look around for something suitable and left. After a long time he returned with a large pile of hay. He didn't tell where he had gotten it, and Camille didn't dare ask for he was convinced that he had taken it from some farmer's haystack. They spread the hay on the ground and laid Manette on it, after John helped her change into dry clothes. She had a high fever, but the boys couldn't do anything except let her drink once in a while and wait.

After they had eaten a bit, Camille went into the forest again to gather more wood and when it grew dark there was enough to keep the fire going until morning, maybe even longer. They agreed to take turns sleeping so that one of them always would be watching

Manette and keep the fire going. John took the first watch. He seated himself close to Manette while Camille curled up on the other side of the fire and fell asleep.

John never forgot that night the rest of his life! It didn't begin too badly because Manette was lying quietly, although she complained about a pain in her chest. A short time later she seemed to have fallen asleep and John was glad. He took it as a sign that she was recovering. Yet, a few hours later when he was considering waking Camille for his turn to watch, her breathing became heavier and she began to talk rapidly. He couldn't understand what she was trying to say and after a few moments she began to scream and cry. She was delirious. That much he understood. Often she tried to stand up and run away, but other times she would crouch down, whimper and beg not to be beaten.

Her yelling woke Camille and it was just in time. John was holding her shoulders to keep her down on the straw, but she was hurting herself by kicking the ground with her legs.

"Hold her legs down," panted John, who could barely hold her. Camille quickly grasped her feet, but she kept fighting until suddenly she had a fit of coughing and quieted down, exhausted.

Desperately the boys looked to each other, knowing that they couldn't do anything. There were no medicines nor did they know how to get them.

"Is she going to die?" Camille asked, crying. John didn't have time to answer for Manette flew up again, and he was just in time to hold her. Her eyes were wide open, but she was unconscious and cried for her mommy. John talked to her and so did Camille, but she didn't listen and kept crying.

Her frenzied fits of fighting lasted the whole night, but were interrupted every time by coughing attacks, which made her temporarily exhausted and calm until a new fit began.

Near dawn a change occurred. She seemed to regain consciousness again. She opened her eyes and looked for a long time at John as if she were trying to remember who he was. Slowly a smile crept onto her face and she whispered, "I am so glad that you are here, John, and that you're helping me."

She grasped his hand, pressed it against her cheek and held it there, laying quietly, faintly smiling. The boys had tears in their eyes for both thought she was going to die. A few moments later her breathing became easier and after having watched her for a long time, John said hesitantly, as if he couldn't believe it, "It looks as if she has fallen asleep!"

It was true. She didn't sleep very peacefully, but she was not delirious anymore. She held on to John's hand and he remained sitting close to her until the day began to lighten, afraid that she might wake up when he moved. Very early in the morning, she let his hand go and opened her eyes widely. She felt very weak and asked what had happened. How had she come into this shack? She didn't remember anything of the previous day. John gave her some water and told her to go to sleep again and to stop thinking and worrying. She closed her eyes obediently. At that moment John was so very tired that he had just enough energy to tell Camille to stay awake before he, too, fell asleep.

For more than a week they stayed in the shack. For the first few days Manette was often delirious, but early the third morning she woke up suddenly feeling much better. From that day on she began to recover quickly, which was to a great extent speeded up by the good care of the boys.

John and Camille became cheerful again and made new plans for the rest of their journey. They realized that they needed more food for they couldn't leave the shack until Manette's condition was sufficiently improved and that could take several more days. Camille came up with the best idea! As they couldn't be far from the city of Amiens, maybe an hour or so, he suggested that he would try to sell the remaining baskets. They could use the money he made to buy enough food to last a good number of days. John agreed fully and gave him some extra money in case he had trouble selling the baskets.

The next morning Camille set out, promising to do his utmost to be back the same night or, if that was impossible, certainly not later than the next day before noon.

John and Manette had a nice, quiet day together. Most of the time Manette slept; but when she was awake, they talked and felt happy with each others company. Both were amazed how much they had to tell each other, for it seemed there was no end to all the events through which they had gone.

At the end of the day she asked John to pray with her and to thank the Lord for her recovery, which he did right away for his heart, also, was full of gratitude.

Afterward she lay for a long time looking quietly and then she told him, timidly, that she had thought she was going to die.

"Weren't you afraid?" John asked, softly.

"Oh, yes, very much at first, but later on I remembered that Mommy once said that the Lord always takes care of you, especially when you are dying. He never forgets His children when they believe in Him and I certainly do! And suddenly I wasn't scared anymore. But, John, I know so very little of the Bible. Can't you tell me more about it so I can learn all the beautiful stories?"

"Do you know what we will do? As soon as we are in Holland we will buy a Bible and then we can read it every day because I don't know that much about it, either."

"But we can't read a Dutch Bible. It may take a very long time before we know Dutch!"

"Oh, no, we'll buy a French one, of course. They must certainly sell them too, I think."

"But, John, that doesn't help me for I don't know how to read. You know I've never been taught. Can you teach me to read?"

"Don't be upset, Manette," he said, for the first time aware that she had never been to school, "as soon as we are in Holland we'll send you directly to school and then you'll see how easy reading is. But now I am going to fix some food and then you go to sleep. Sleep and good food will make you healthy again."

It was true, he thought while preparing food. She was so young when they took her to Paris that nobody would expect her to remember most of the Bible stories Mother had told us. Yet, she had not given in to Madame Jordan! She must really be courageous or could it be that the Lord makes you brave so that you won't deny Him? He wished that he knew somebody whom he could ask such questions. Wouldn't it be nice if he could talk about all these things with a real minister?

The next day around noon, Camille returned. When he was near the shack, he suddenly stopped and sniffed. What a delicious smell, he thought, just as if John was roasting some meat!

He was right, for John was broiling a rabbit over the open fire. It had struck him the previous day that the thicket abounded with rabbits. Cautiously, he had placed a few snares on some trails, like his father had taught him. In the morning he had found a big rabbit in one of them.

For Camille, who had never lived in a forest, it was a great idea. Imagine, to be able to catch rabbits with a snare! Besides, who wouldn't be surprised when he smelled the delicious food John had prepared?

"Your rabbit is, indeed, a great surprise," he said laughing, "but I have also a great surprise for you, or rather, for Manette!

He opened his bag and first showed them all the food he had with him. They were astonished when they saw the large quantity he had purchased. He must have used all the money, they thought. But that wasn't true at all. He laughed mysteriously when he took a folded bundle from the bag and threw it to Manette before they could see what it was.

"A special present for you, Manette," he beamed.

He laughed even louder at their astonished looks when they unfolded the package and saw that it was a woolen coat, somewhat worn out but well usable and warm.

"How did you get that?" John and Manette called, both at the same moment.

"Well, let me tell the whole story from the very beginning. In the first place, we are slightly more than three quarters of an hour walking from Amiens and I arrived there rather early. It wasn't difficult to sell the baskets. The rest of the day I looked around, for I wanted to make some extra money so that I could purchase a warm dress or something for Manette. I expected that it would cost more money than I had received for the baskets. John, you had given me some money, but I didn't want to use it. I wanted to give Manette a present bought from my own money. Since I wasn't very successful in making money, I made up my mind, at last, to go to a tailor. Maybe I could buy a warm skirt and if it was too expensive, well, then I'd have to use John's money. I knew that I didn't really have enough, but I felt that I could, at least, give it a try.

"I asked people where I could find a tailor and they directed me to a tiny house where a hunchbacked tailor sat cross-legged on a table, sewing diligently. Of course, I had no chance at all of purchasing a dress for everything was far too expensive and I didn't know what to do. At last I saw this coat hanging on a nail in the corner of the room and asked how much he wanted for it. The tailor laughed and said that he wouldn't sell such an old coat. As a matter of fact, he was still using it for it was woven from good wool. During our small talk he asked what I was doing in Amiens. I told him that I am a traveling basket-maker. He glanced at me disdainfully and said that he didn't believe a word of it, that I was far too young for such a job. I became angry and told him that I could prove it, provided I had the proper materials to work with.

"In the meantime his wife had come in. She seemed to believe me for she asked if I could fix their baby's cradle. She took me inside and showed it to me. It was woven from very thin twigs, with one side all broken up. I don't understand how that ever happened and she never told me. After I said that the repair would be rather easy, the tailor climbed down from the table and took me outside the city limits to a spot where a lot of similar twigs grew. We cut them down and took them to his house. In the meantime, it had become so dark that I left, promising them I would return today. I found a sleeping place outside the city in a dry ditch. Brrr, it was cold, sleeping in the open! I'd rather use a nice, warm haystack anytime!

"Today, early in the morning, I went back to the tailor and repaired the cradle. Last night we hadn't discussed the price, and when he asked today how much he had to pay, I just pointed with my finger to the coat. First he shrugged his shoulders, but his wife supported me. She said that giving that old coat as payment was far cheaper than giving money. And so I got it!"

All three laughed. Camille was really a smart fellow, and the coat was nice and warm, well suited for Manette!

They stayed another week in the shack until Manette felt well enough to walk a few hours a day. John and Camille knew how important it was to be on their way again. A longer stay for her benefit might mean that they would not be able to reach Holland before wintertime, which was of the greatest importance.

While in Amiens, Camille had used his time well and had gathered a lot of useful information. It was impossible to cross the border easily for soldiers watched it continuously. However, some people living close to the border were willing to guide people across using unknown smuggler's paths, provided they were well paid for it!

John felt that they could try to find such a guide for he owned a Louis d'or, remember?

They couldn't walk fast during the first days because Manette was still too weak, but gradually her health improved until she was as strong as the boys.

After a week they noticed in the morning that the air began to smell differently, a strong salty smell, and in the afternoon they saw, unexpectedly, the sea!

They never had seen such a sight! Nothing but a large stretch of continuously moving water and far away a few small fishing boats. For a long time they stood enjoying this beautiful but also strange view. John was the first to come back to earth by making a simple observation.

"At least it makes it easy for us to find our way. As long as we follow the coastline we can't miss Holland, for it also borders the sea!"

18

CAMILLE JUMPS INTO THE SEA

It wasn't easy following the coastline for the road didn't always stay close to the water. Sometimes it bent sharply inland, and when that happened John and Camille worried that it would lead them too far away from the sea and they would get lost. Happily, the road always returned to the coast, and then they were glad, indeed, to see the sea with its beautiful rolling waves again. They were quite sure they were going in the proper direction as long as they could see the water line.

They were in an excellent mood. The end of their traveling couldn't be far off, they felt. Sure, the last leg of their journey might take more time than expected, but it would be short in comparison with the many weeks they had been under way. Their troubles weren't over yet and the hardest part, crossing the border, was still to come, but that morning they couldn't have cared less.

The weather was perfect, although growing colder. The wind off the sea left a salty flavor in their mouths, which tasted particularly good. Besides, there was so much to see that they often stopped a moment to have a good look at the beautiful scenery.

The coast consisted of white-gray rocks, worn smooth by the pounding waves. Seagulls, the beautiful birds of the sea, were everywhere. Far off the coastline they sometimes saw fishing boats bravely setting their course to the fishing grounds, and once they even saw a small rowboat with two boys in it.

For most of that morning, the road had been quite far above sea level, but gradually wound its way down to the water's edge again, not always to the water's edge, though. Sometimes it went across rocks rather far from the water line, so that a sandy beach was formed between the road and the sea. At other times, however, the road came so close to the water that the froth of the waves flew into their faces. It wasn't a lonely road either for once in a while they saw other people walking along the path, mostly women and children.

Late in the afternoon, an old man came walking toward them. A little girl of about six years old was with him, skipping and running around and having a wonderful time. In dangerous spots, the old man called her and held her hand, but as soon as she saw an opportunity to escape, she let his hand go and darted to the other side of the road. A few times she picked up shells and, of course, she had to show every one of them to the old man, who pretended to be very much interested. Other times, she found other fascinating things like seaweed, which she would grab and hold in her hands while skipping along.

They were less than a hundred feet away from the old man when it happened! The road curved again close to the water and he called the little girl, intending to hold her hand. She came running, but at the very moment that she lifted her hand to grab him, she stumbled. How it exactly happened nobody could later recall, but she made a few awkward turns and slipped down the side of the road over the edge into the water. A loud cry and a splash . . . and that was all!

The man, who was carrying a net with some fish over his shoulder, dropped it, threw himself on his belly and tried to reach the girl, but it was in vain. The water was at least three feet below the road and his arms were far too short to reach her. Besides, the child was under water and couldn't be seen. A moment later she came to the surface and opened her mouth as if she wanted to yell, but not knowing how to swim, went under again.

However, even though she couldn't swim, Camille could. He ran to the spot where she had disappeared, and without thinking, leaped into the sea. Brrr, he shivered with cold, but didn't have time to think about it. He had to be ready when the girl came up again. Yes, he saw her dress faintly underneath the water, but this time she didn't quite make it to the surface. Half a foot under water she stopped struggling and began to sink again.

Camille, who wasn't close enough to grab her, swam like a madman into her direction and dived under where he had seen her last. Deep down below the surface he saw her dress vaguely, grabbed it and pulled her with him to the surface. She didn't stir and felt lifeless like a big, wet doll. Suddenly he became terrified, wondering if he had been too late.

A few forceful strokes brought him to the shore where the old man, John, and Manette stood, petrified. Camille pushed her up so that John could get hold of her and, with the help of the old man,

151

pulled her quickly out of the water and onto the road. Camille himself had more trouble climbing onto the shore, but managed eventually with the help of John, who saw him struggling.

In the meantime, the old man had taken his granddaughter, who seemed to be dead, in his arms. Nobody knew exactly what to do, but since she must have had a great deal of water in her lungs, he held her upside down, desperately hoping that the water would stream out. It helped. A large gulp of seawater came out of her mouth. The man shook her vehemently, and again she vomited dirty water. Then she opened her eyes and began to cry. He hugged her and kissed her, glad that she was alive. Without more ado, he said to the children, "Come." He then began to run as fast as his old legs could carry him, back along the path from where he had come. The children followed him, after Manette had the excellent idea of grabbing the net with the fish.

The man soon discovered that he wasn't strong enough to keep running with the girl in his arms. Without stopping he turned to John, who was running beside him and handed her over. John took her and laid her comfortably against his shoulder so that he could carry her with ease.

When Camille began to run he felt exhausted. Those few minutes in the water had taken more out of him than a whole week of work. Running was good for him, though, for his tiredness grew less and he even warmed up a bit.

Ten minutes later, they reached a tiny house, the old man's home, and went inside. The little girl was conscious, but frightfully cold. Her grandfather, who saw the child shivering, asked Manette to undress her and dry her with a towel, rubbing as hard as possible to make her warm. In the meantime, he took care of the fire, which was smoldering in the open fireplace. Soon it was flaming again, and the chilly room became comfortably warm.

Next, the grandfather heated a few large rocks in the fire, wrapped them in old rags and placed them close to the girl, who Manette had already put to bed. The warmth of the fire and the hot rocks made her so drowsy that she fell asleep at once.

The man had watched her anxiously while taking care of the fire. Sighing with relief, he turned to the boys and said gratefully, "I think that my little girl will be all right pretty soon. I don't know how I ever can thank you for your help. I can't swim and if you hadn't jumped into the water, she would surely have drowned!"

Camille blushed shyly. He had dried himself as well as possible and was now keeping himself busy with laying all his wet clothing around the fire. He felt embarrassed that the old man was so thankful for the little thing he had done. After all, he could swim like an otter and anybody who could swim so well would, of course, have done the same thing. He muttered that it was a waste of time to talk about such a simple thing for he was sure that John would have done the same had he been fast enough.

"Sure," laughed John, who was proud of his friend, "but I wasn't quick enough. You were!"

"Well, don't start a fight." said the man, smiling, "I am thankful, you better believe it! I haven't even introduced myself. I am Desjardins. Who are you and where do you hail from?"

The boys and Manette told him their names and John added that they came from Paris and were itinerant basket makers because they had to earn a living for themselves.

"So, nobody is expecting you tonight, eh?" the man said pleasantly. "Excellent, for then you can stay here! Come on, John, you can help me prepare our supper by cleaning the fish, please. You have done it before, haven't you? In the meantime I'll do the rest!"

Grandfather Desjardins was a very nice person to talk with. He had two married sons, who lived half an hour further down the coast. Little Suzette, his grandchild, was the child of his daughter, who died a few years ago. Her father was a fisherman who worked together with his sons on their own boat. Since her father had no more children and most of the time went fishing, the girl stayed here with her grandfather. Tomorrow night he expected his son-in-law to come home, and it would be very nice if they could stay long enough so that he could thank them personally.

It was very cozy in the room. The fire gave out a soft, reddish light, which made them all feel at home. After a good meal of bread and fish, Grandfather seated himself in a chair before the fire, and the children sat down on the ground, close to him.

Hearing her grandfather's voice, the little girl soon awoke, got out of bed and climbed on his knee. First she listened quietly to him, but soon she was bored and asked with her most winning smile if Grandpa couldn't tell her a nice fairy tale. He only laughed and teasingly pretended that he had forgotten all the beautiful stories. When she kept asking, he told her a fantastic tale about a mermaid who had been naughty.

After he had finished, the children asked him about his life on the sea and he narrated all kinds of humorous tales from his life at sea. Gradually his voice changed, though, and became more serious when he described all the difficulties that the fishermen have to overcome to catch enough fish to make a living.

He explained that the sea is very beautiful but also treacherous and can never be trusted. Heavy storms and waves as high as houses can ruin in one moment all the fishermen's sails and the nets, his most precious possessions, and often he can barely even save his life. He told them of cruel pirates who sometimes succeeded in seizing their boats. Merciless, they hanged or drowned the captured fishermen who were unwilling to join them. Fishing for nights on end without catching anything worthwhile happened frequently, but every once in a while they caught such an enormous quantity that they could go home after one single night fishing.

At the end of the evening, John asked him a question that had been on his mind all the time.

"Have you ever seen the galleys on which convicts have to row?"

The face of the old man changed suddenly. Somber, he looked a few moments at John and asked who had told him that he had been forced to row on a galley for two years. The boys, very much surprised, denied vehemently having talked with anybody about him. How could they when they didn't even know him until a few hours ago?

One moment the man looked dumbfounded, but then he began to smile.

"You are right, of course! I forgot that I haven't known you all my life. You look so familiar that I can hardly believe that I saw you for the first time this afternoon.

"Yes, for two years I was on the galleys! It happened a long time ago when I was still young. My wife was alive and my children were very small. That year we didn't have much success. We hadn't caught a fair amount of fish during the whole season and were nearly starving. After several months of nothing but ill fortune, we suddenly had an excellent catch. At that time I was fishing with my neighbors. We all owned the boat and divided the profits equally. Imagine, at last we had caught sufficient fish to feed our families. We came home in high spirits, not because we had so much but because it was enough to live on for a few weeks.

"When we came ashore, we saw the tax collector coming down the road. He wanted to know how many fish we had caught. We hadn't been able to pay our taxes during the last weeks and now that fellow told us that we had to pay it instantly. If we didn't he would sell our fish to get the money we owed.

"When I heard him and realized that all our toiling had been in vain, I became raging mad. I hit him so hard in his face that he turned head over heels and tumbled down over a few rocks. He wasn't dead, but I kept hammering him down until he had two black eyes and was missing his front teeth. Well, he was really a sight, for the rocks had cut his face rather badly, too. My friends held me so that I couldn't attack him anymore, and he was taken home, yelling that he would make me regret my assault. And that is precisely what he did!

"I was brought to court the next morning, and the judge sent me to the galleys for two years. Those were the worst years of my life. With a little money you could buy extra food and send letters home, but neither I nor my wife had any money. So, I was hungry all those years and never heard from my wife and children. Every day we had to row continuously for ten hours and the food was terrible. After two years of this slave labor I came home a skeleton."

The old man remained quiet after having told this story, thinking about that part of his life. At last John dared to ask one more question.

"Were there any Huguenots on the galleys and how were they treated?"

"Yes, there were, and they were far worse off than anyone else. No decent fellow would treat his dog as mean as these poor men were treated. Slaves on a galley are often very embittered, just like I was when sent there, and for that reason lots of evil occurs. This is understandable when you realize that nearly all the rowers on the galleys are the worst of criminals. The Huguenots were surely no criminals, and they were far different from anybody I know. I admired them during my time on the galleys, and even today, I respect them immensely. They wanted to convert me, but that was, of course, nonsense. However, I would never have survived those years without them. Every time I was disheartened, they encouraged me and once, when I intended to throw myself overboard, one of them talked so long with me that I didn't do it.

"Yet, everything was far worse for them than for us. Our food was very bad, but their food was spoiled. We were beaten, but they were beaten far more and much harder. Nobody ever cared for our sick ones, but we were at least left alone. Their sick ones were thrown down and left to die in the most horrible places. Everybody was always amazed that they didn't give in, for they could get free with three simple words.[17] They would be set free in the next harbor, would get new clothing and could go home as soon as they promised to reunite with the Roman Church. No one ever recanted and they continued rowing. They were willing to risk everything to obey God, Who, they said, forbade them to give in. Who knows? Maybe they were right.

"They formed a kind of secret club together[18] not a real club, of course, for that couldn't be done. I guess, you could call it a kind of agreement to help each other as much as possible. They encouraged their "brothers," as they called themselves, a great deal, especially when they became afraid that one of them was willing to give in by becoming a Romanist. I heard from these Huguenots that everybody can pray directly to God and they themselves did it frequently. Often they sang together, not loud because that was forbidden, but just humming to themselves. For months I was chained to one of them. He told me that they were singing Psalms that were written in the Bible. Sometimes he recited them to me softly, and I have learned a few of them by heart. The most amazing thing was that they also prayed for the slave drivers who beat them, and when they prayed they talked just like a child talks to his Father. I will never forget that! The one to which I was chained, always prayed in common French and never used a single Latin word. At first I thought that he was one of their priests — ministers they call them — because he knew so much of the Bible, but he told me that he was just a poor tailor. There were few ministers left, he said, because most of them were imprisoned.

"A very surprising thing happened just before I was released. On board we had a Roman priest, as is common on ships of war. One day, when one of the Huguenots was being whipped he went to the slave driver, grasped the whip and forbade him to whip one of his brothers. It was reported to the commander and very soon the priest was interrogated. He admitted being so impressed by the attitude of the Huguenots that he had begun to study the Bible himself to

---

[17] Only three French words were needed: *Je me réunis* (I reunite)
[18] This association, called "Believers on the Galleys" was formed in 1699.

discover from where they got their courage. At last he understood that God was at their side, and that he was wrong, a priest of a false church. After much praying and reading he had repented and knew now that he also belonged to Christ and should be a witness for Christ!

"The very same day he was chained to a rower's seat and was treated far worse than the other Huguenots. Yet, I have never seen anyone in my life happier than he. He said that he was privileged to be allowed to suffer for Christ's sake.[19] Since that time I have admired the Huguenots, although I never met one after I left the galley. There aren't many of them in this part of the country or perhaps they are in hiding."[20]

During his story, Manette and John had become more and more pale, and now Manette couldn't keep from crying. The old man looked at her and said, trying to comfort her, "Don't cry anymore, sweetheart. It is a long time ago that I was there and I came back, right?"

John, who had also been trying to force back his tears, couldn't stand it any longer and blurted out, "Our Daddy is also on the galleys. We haven't seen him for years." He stopped, embarrassed that he had given away their secret to a stranger.

Astonished, the old man jumped up as if bitten by a viper. "Your father is on the galleys? That is why you asked about it! Why is he there? What has he done and for how long is he committed?"

John, seeing no way out, admitted that his father was a Huguenot and it didn't take long to tell Mr. Desjardins all the important events of their flight to Holland — how long they had been on their way and that they were afraid they would not be able to cross the border, and much more.

Obviously, John and Manette were upset at hearing all these bad things about the galleys. Camille and Grandfather tried to comfort them and gradually they grew calm again.

In the meantime it had become rather late, and the old man stopped all further discussion by telling them that they all had to go to bed. He piled a few old fishing nets on top of each other in the corner of the room and put a blanket over it. Manette, he said, could sleep in the same bed as Suzette, the boys could sleep in his bed, and he

---

[19] This is a true story. The name of this chaplain was Jean Bion.
[20] The situation on the galleys was far worse than Grandfather told.

would sleep on the fishing nets. The boys protested in vain that they could sleep on the nets, but grandfather insisted that they should take the bed.

A short time later everybody was asleep except Camille and John, who whispered together for a long time.

GRANDFATHER SHOWS
HIS GRATITUDE

John woke up early the next morning. The first thing he heard was the sound of somebody moving around in the room. It was Desjardins, who had built up the fire and hung a pot over it in which he was boiling porridge. He was now sweeping the floor. John jumped out of his bed and said softly, so that the girls and Camille who were still asleep, would not wake up, "Good morning, Grandpa. Couldn't you sleep that you are cleaning up so early?"

"Also good morning to you. Yes, old people don't need as much sleep as young ones and therefore I am always up rather early. I was just wondering who would wake up first and I'm glad it is you for I have to ask you something, but it can wait till you have washed yourself at the well. Here is a clean rag to dry yourself with. I have no towels, but a rag works just as well!"

John laughed and went outside. When he came back, the old man gave him a bowl of porridge and sat down on the edge of the table while John was eating.

"John, it seems to me that you are more or less the leader of you three children and that is right, for you are the oldest. I'd like to talk with you before the others wake up. You told me that you are Huguenots, fleeing to Holland. Don't be afraid that I will betray you for I told you of my experiences on the galleys and that I respect the Huguenots. Besides, I am thankful that Camille saved little Suzette from drowning.

"You mentioned that you want to be in Holland before the winter starts and that you must be on your way again as soon as possible. I would appreciate it if you did not leave today but stay until tomorrow. I don't ask this for my own sake or for Suzette's father. I have another reason that I don't want to mention. I've the impression that Camille won't like the idea that my son-in-law will thank him but that can't be helped! I know that Camille and Manette will do as you tell them. What do you think? Can't you do me this small favor and stay one day?"

John wasn't sure what to think of the suggestion. He trusted Desjardins absolutely, but it was rather odd that the old man insisted on their staying another day. Well, John decided, he was a very friendly man who was probably trying to show his gratitude by making sure that they were rested and well fed before leaving again! After all, one day more or less wouldn't make too much of a difference, even if it was late in the season. Without giving it another thought, he accepted the kind invitation.

Grandfather gave a sigh of relief and said, smiling, "Fine, but I've more to ask. I want your help for little Suzette. My sons and son-in-law will come home late in the afternoon or early at night. It is the last trip of this season and they have to run the boat on the beach near the village so that it will be stored safely during the winter. They need my help, as usual.

"Every year Suzette goes with me, but this time I'd like her to stay home after her wet adventure yesterday. Would you be willing to take care of her while I'm away? You don't have to stay inside the house all day. You can take her with you if you want to go for a walk. Do not wait for me tonight. I have no idea how late I'll be back. It is better to go to bed early so that you will be well rested when you take off again, tomorrow."

Without hesitating John promised to help and then Grandfather suggested to wake the others.

Twenty minutes later everybody was dressed and happily engaged in talking and eating. After breakfast they all went out for a walk and when they came back, the old man showed them how to repair the nets.

Late in the afternoon Grandfather went to the village. Before leaving he told them what to cook for supper and again told them not to wait for him but to go to bed early!

The boys felt as if they had just gone to bed when both woke up at the same time. Heavy steps and some mumbling of dark voices could be heard outside. Having grown accustomed to dangerous and unexpected situations, they leaped out of bed. Not fully awake, John wondered who that could be. Was it Grandpa with his sons or strangers who had lost their way? The door opened and three men entered the room, but it was too dark to see who they were. One of them carried a lantern.

"You are awake?" Grandfather's voice sounded surprised. "I expected you all to be asleep, but this is far better. Wait, let me first light the fire!"

The man with the lantern went to the fireplace and opened the lantern. He took the burning candle out of it, and lighted the wood in the fireplace.

"Dad, which one is the courageous boy who rescued Suzette?" one of the men asked. Grandfather pointed to Camille and said, "That is the water rat who bravely jumped into the sea and grasped our little darling."

"Camille, I don't know how to show my thankfulness," the man said, putting his hands on Camille's shoulders in a friendly gesture.

"Oh, no," he laughed suddenly, "I am wrong. I know precisely how to show my gratitude. That is the very reason for my coming tonight. Father told us that you are anxious to go to Holland and we plan to take you in our boat! Hurry, get the girls and dress quickly for we have no time to lose. We brought the boat as close to here as possible, but we must wait another twelve hours if we don't hurry. High tide is already coming in, and we have to be aboard when it is at its highest. We can't leave at low tide because the boat is too high on the beach and we haven't enough strength to push it into the water. Dress yourselves as warm as you can, for it is cold on the water. Where are the girls? Tell them to hurry also!"

Delighted, the boys hardly knew what to say. Such a great, unexpected surprise! To be in Holland in such a short time! It was incredible!

The noise and the sound of the exited voices had aroused the girls. Manette, understanding that they must hurry, began to dress Suzette, who was still half asleep, when she suddenly saw her father. She jumped out of bed and into his arms and, laughing, cried out, "I knew that you would come home tonight. Grandpa told me so."

After hugging the girl, her father told her to dress quickly.

"I have a surprise for you. Didn't I promise to take you sailing when you are a big girl? Well, if you are big enough to dress in a hurry, we'll take you with us when we go sailing tonight."

Nothing more needed to be added, for in a jubilant, nervous hurry she grasped her clothes and hustled them on.

The children were ready in the shortest possible time and soon were walking with the men along the shore to the boat. When they arrived, John heard one of the men mutter that they were just in time. Not understanding why that was so, he looked at the boat and saw that it was rather small. It was partly pulled onto the beach and was resting with its bow on the sand and its stern in the water.

Climbing aboard wasn't easy, but with the help of the fishermen even the girls managed.

The man who had remained aboard when the others had gone to fetch the children, said, "I began to wonder if you would be back in time, but happily you made it. We can sail in half an hour!"

It was still dark and the men took them into a small cabin that was illuminated by two candles. They had never seen such a funny, small room. Nets were hanging from the walls, and there were several unknown things. They were surprised to see how small the nets were. Low benches stood against the walls and everybody sat down except the girls. They were too excited to sit quietly and kept going from one side of the cabin to the other side, looking at all the strange things.

"Why are these nets hanging on the wall," Manette asked.

"Those aren't nets. They are our beds," said one of the men smiling, who heard her question in spite of all the noisy talking. "At night we hook them up to the wall and then you can sleep in them. Look here, this end we move over this hook and the other side goes to the hook in that wall and now, you girls, can sleep in it the rest of tonight. Tomorrow will be a very long day for you and I doubt that you slept too much today."

While he was talking, his hands had been busy attaching a hammock to the wall hooks and now he told the girls to climb into it. Manette, delighted with this unusual bed, grabbed one of the sides of the hammock and tried to hoist herself in it. Before she knew what happened it turned around and only her holding onto the sides saved her from falling down altogether, although her knees hit the floor painfully hard. Everybody laughed. Before she could make another effort, John and Camille tried it. They also did their utmost, but couldn't figure out how to do it easily. The hammock turned around every time they tried it. After many trials, all of them managed somehow to climb into a hammock, but had to admit shamefacedly that they didn't have the hang of it.

One of the fishermen who couldn't stop laughing, seeing their clumsy efforts, pushed the children aside, grasped both sides of the hammock at the same time, and swung himself into it.

"That is the way," he said.

The boys tried to imitate him, and after some practicing they could do it also, but of course not as fast as the fisherman. The girls couldn't master the trick at all and had to be lifted inside the hammock by grandfather.

It is surprising how good a hammock feels when you are tired. The girls were very comfortable and said that it felt so good that they weren't going to leave their bed for a long time.

While they were having all this fun, time had gone by, and they heard the man who had stayed aboard call for help. The men, who were waiting for this call, went directly to him. John and Camille followed. When they came on deck, they saw to their great surprise that the boat was completely surrounded by water. Now they understood why they had waited for high tide, but didn't think that the water was high enough, for the ship was still resting on the sand.

"Well, everything is ready! We can leave now," Grandfather said good-naturedly.

"He must be joking," John whispered to Camille. Grandfather had overheard him and smiled.

"What's the matter, John?"

"We are still sitting in the sand. We can't move, Grandpa!"

"That doesn't matter, my boy. We just have to help the old boat a little to get her floating again, that is all. You boys come with me. I need some strong arms."

The men went to the mast and made preparations to hoist the mainsail. The boys followed the old man to the rear of the ship where they saw a capstan, a sort of winch from which a cable disappeared overboard into the sea.

"Let's try to pull that cable in. An anchor is tied to the other end of the cable and we better have it on board before leaving," grandfather said with a mischievous twinkle in his eyes.

The boys, enthusiastic and glad that they could help, began to turn the capstan and soon the cable became taut until at last, it didn't move anymore in spite of their hard pushing. The old man encouraged them to push harder still and he himself even lent a hand, but it was impossible to move the handle until the other fishermen came to help. They all pushed with all their might and all at once they felt slight vibration on the ship. After more even harder pushing, they perceived that the ship was moving toward the sea, and a short time later they were afloat.

"Careful now," grandfather warned, for turning the capstan made them float slowly toward the place where the anchor was buried in the sand. Then the fishermen easily brought the anchor aboard with John and Camille's help. The wind began to fill the sails . . . and they sailed away from the shore toward the open sea to Holland, to their freedom!

The children enjoyed their first trip on the water tremendously. They walked all over the ship and asked the fishermen hundreds of questions, which they answered patiently. One of them explained the difficulty of finding good fishing grounds and taught them the names of many things aboard. He even showed them how to make different knots in a rope and how they were used.

Very little work needed to be done during their trip. Once in a while they had to change their direction slightly or the sails had to be readjusted to take advantage of the wind, but that was all. Grandfather especially had nothing to do and the children sat with him during the afternoon, all enjoying the nice weather and the beautiful calm sea.

After a long period of sitting, John asked grandfather if he ever had been in Holland, and before they knew it the old man, who loved to tell stories, began to talk about the Dutch.

He had never been in Holland himself, but he had seen the Dutch often. As a matter of fact, every sailor knew them. They had so many ships and sailors that you could always find a few of them in any harbor around the world. He had heard that they had as many fishing boats as all the other countries together. That was, maybe, an exaggeration but they certainly had a lot. It was also well known that they owned a great many other ships, which they used for their extensive trade. They sailed all over the world, north and south, east and west, to India and America, even to Africa and China.

Holland was a very small country that didn't even have a king like most other countries. A prince ruled them. He was a courageous man, as everybody knew. Long ago, twenty-five years or so ago, France and England both fought the Dutch at the same time, but couldn't overpower them. King Louis had sent a very large army with famous generals, the best in the world, and England used its large navy in the North Sea, but it didn't work. That very same prince had managed to stop the army, and the Dutch had swept the English Navy back into England. During that war, when everything

165

appeared to be lost, the English advised him to surrender. He told them that a good way of not seeing the downfall of his country was to be killed while fighting on its last fortress.

Many years later Grandfather himself had seen an impressive manifestation of the Dutch sea power. They were just on their way to Dogger Bank, a shallow part of the North Sea, which is a very good fishing area. One morning they woke up and found themselves surrounded by an incredibly large number of warships. He had never seen so many ships together in his whole life. The sea was crowded with all these magnificent ships wherever you looked. It was the prince on his way to conquer England. Apparently, the English had asked for his help for they detested their king, who had reduced the power of the Protestants. The prince, who also was a Protestant, was willing to do everything in his power to help their cause. He sailed to England with his mighty navy and chased the English king away. After the victory, the English had made him their king and he still ruled England. His name was now King William of Orange.[21]

Holland was rather small, but it was immensely rich and all the people worked hard. It was surely the country of freedom for everybody was welcome. One of the odd things in Holland was that those Dutch with good government positions and the wealthy merchants spoke French rather than Dutch.

However, most of the Dutch were rather crude, especially the sailors. When they sail into a harbor you can be sure that the innkeepers will make a lot of money for they love to drink a lot. However, it means also that many brawls will be started for they love fighting when they're drunk and do it at the slightest provocation.

John, Camille, and Manette listened spellbound to all these stories and kept asking questions, which Grandfather answered willingly and so the afternoon passed quickly.

Grandfather stopped telling his stories at sundown and it became somewhat chilly. He made supper and then the children were sent to bed. They slept well that night for the salty sea breeze had made them so sleepy that they could hardly keep their eyes open when they were lying in their hammocks. The calm, monotonous movement of the waves rocked the hammocks slowly so that it felt as if they were nicely cradled in the arms of their mothers.

---

[21] King William of Orange (William III) did not like England, but needed it to form a large coalition against the Roman Catholic King Louis XIV. He expressed his motives well by the slogan on the banners of his war ships, during his cross-over to England, "I Will Maintain the Liberty of England and the Protestant Religion."

20

DUTCH HOSPITALITY

Early the following morning, John, Camille, and Manette stood on a sandy beach waving goodbye to their friends, who were slowly sailing away. The fishermen didn't like the idea of sailing into a Dutch harbor and had rowed them to a desolate part of the Dutch coast, where they were put ashore.

The land looked far different from what the children had expected. They stood on a wide stretch of fine, white sand, which changed further inland into a row of sand hills. All kinds of whole and broken shells were mixed in with the sand and it felt warm and good to their bare feet.

Grandfather and Suzette's father had brought them ashore. They told them that a half-hour walk to the south would bring them to a large city, called Vlissingen. They couldn't get lost as long as they followed the coastline. After a few more friendly words, they embraced the children, thanked them anew for saving little Suzette, and then went into the rowboat and returned to their ship.

The children watched until the ship disappeared beyond the horizon. They were still looking to that distant spot when John said, "It's a pity that we probably never will see them again. Let's never forget how friendly they have been and how much they helped us. Let's hope that in a few years it will be safe for us again in France so that we can visit them."

Somewhat timidly, he added that they must be thankful to the Lord that they were at last in Holland and suggested to thank Him at the very spot where they had landed. Camille and Manette agreed wholeheartedly, and so all three knelt on the sand while John, aloud, in simple words gave thanks to the Lord for His great goodness, which had made everything so well.

After their prayer, they were silent for a long time. It was difficult to understand that the worst part of their journey was over, even as they felt the sand of Holland underneath their feet. At last Camille broke the silence with a cheerful smile.

"What do you think? Wouldn't it be better to walk to that city rather than stay here in the sand gathering dust?"

"Why don't you try to catch us, slowpoke," John called even before Camille had finished talking. Grasping Manette's hand, he raced along the beach with her. Camille, taken by surprise, did not lose time, though, and went after them as fast as his legs could carry him. Obviously, they could not keep up the race long and gradually slowed down until they were walking at their ease southward along the beach with the happy feeling that now all their difficulties and troubles were over.

It took them a little more than an hour before they were in Vlissingen. Most of the time during their walk they had discussed what would be the best thing to do next. Grandfather had told them that a great number of Huguenots were living in Holland. They felt that one of them would certainly help them if they could find him. But they did not have the faintest idea what to do to locate help. It was impossible to ask the people in the streets if they were Huguenots for they could not even speak their language! They were really at a loss about what to do. At last, just before entering the city, John decided to look for a decent inn and to ask there about the Huguenots.

They had seen a good number of villages and cities and even Paris during their travels, but this city was fascinating, different from any French city they knew. Most of the houses were built of brick, and the people in the streets were well dressed and well fed. The streets were busy and everybody seemed to be hard at work. The city looked prosperous and rich, the children thought.

Without knowing it, they walked in the same direction as most people in the streets and so, unexpectedly, arrived at the harbor. It was for them a spectacular sight! Amazed, they saw the great number of boats. It seemed to them as if all the ships of the whole world were gathered together in this tiny harbor, small fishing boats as well as giant sea castles, which sailed to the ends of the earth. Everywhere people were busy with loading and unloading or with other jobs. A great number of sailors with open shirts and careless attitudes were in the streets, mixing with the crowd.

The children, although a little afraid of the buzzing around of all these people, were very much interested in all that was going on.

Unfortunately, they had a lot of trouble with the children in the city, who had discovered that they were foreigners. Soon a few began to follow them, yelling and ridiculing their clothing and way of talking. At first, John, Camille, and Manette ignored them, but when the number of children increased to a rather large group they became more and more a great nuisance. Camille, furious, turned around a few times and yelled that they must go home but when they heard his French they mockingly imitated his words and began to follow them even closer.

At last, when even John was getting angry, unexpected help came in the shape of a gentleman, who apparently saw that Manette was nearly in tears. He dispersed the children with a few harsh words and addressed John in Dutch. John obviously didn't understand it and replied in French by asking directions to an inn where they could buy a meal. The man shrugged his shoulders and began to walk away when Camille saved the situation. He drew the gentleman's attention by grasping one of his sleeves. Camille then imitated eating by pointing to his mouth and pretending to chew. Next he rubbed his stomach with such a satisfied grin on his face that all of them began to laugh. The gentleman also smiled and apparently understood Camille's mimics for he took John's arm and brought them to a house where a large sign with an anchor painted on it hung above the door. He opened the door, pushed the three children through it and left.

They saw a large room, the barroom of an inn where a few men were sitting around a large table, drinking beer. One of them stood up, came over to them and said something. Thinking he must be the innkeeper, John asked for a meal in French hoping that the man would understand, but that wasn't so. The man simply shrugged his shoulders and moved his hands to indicate that he did not understand John. Again they had to resort to sign language to tell the innkeeper that they wanted something to eat. He replied by rubbing his thumb against his forefinger as if he was counting money. Its meaning was clear enough and John reassured him directly by taking money from his pocket and showing it to the innkeeper, who nodded pleasantly and took them to a table in the rear of the room.

Barely able to control their laughter, the children seated themselves. It was funny not being able to understand the people and to be forced to use sign language. They would have roared with laughter if they only had dared.

"But how can we find out where the Huguenots live?" John wondered aloud, feeling unsure of himself.

"Well, let's try to explain to the innkeeper that we are Huguenots by showing your Huguenot cross," Camille suggested.

"Yes, that might work. What else can we do, anyway?" John said hesitantly.

Indeed, Holland must be a very rich country considering the large quantity of food the innkeeper served: wheat bread, eggs, ham and beer. It looked appetizing, and all at once the children realized how hungry they were in spite of the good meals on the ship.

Before they began to eat, though, John told the innkeeper slowly and distinctly that they were Huguenots and showed him the Huguenot cross.

First, the innkeeper looked at him with a kind of smile on his face, not understanding a single word of John's story but when he heard the word Huguenot and saw the coin, suddenly he paid close attention to the unintelligible sounds. After John stopped talking, he pointed his finger at them and asked, "Huguenots?"

"Yes, yes," the children hastened to answer and they nodded so hard that their heads nearly rolled off their shoulders. The man muttered something softly. The children, of course, didn't understand it, else they would have heard him say "poor children." Rumors about the fate of the Huguenots in France could be heard everywhere in Holland and he understood that they had fled France and therefore needed help.

With a cheerful smile he made a gesture to the food indicating that they should start eating. He stroked Manette's hair a moment and left them, still smiling. The children weren't sure if he had understood them but they began their meal, anyway. There was time enough after the meal to worry about their next step.

During the meal the innkeeper didn't appear any more because he was too busy serving the other guests, but a girl made sure that they got as much as they wanted. When they had eaten their fill, they signalled to the girl that they were ready. She cleared the table and disappeared. The next half hour nothing happened while they patiently waited for the innkeeper to ask for his money. He didn't come, though, and at last John became impatient.

"The innkeeper seems to have forgotten us," he said. "I'll go and pay him now. Let's then look around outside for somebody who speaks or understands French. Maybe we'll have more success at the harbor. Some sailors may at least understand it a little."

Camille did not agree. He felt that they should stay overnight in the inn and try again tomorrow because they were tired and had to sleep somewhere.

John didn't even listen to him. He stood up, took some money out of his pocket and went to the other end of the room where the innkeeper was. Camille and Manette had no choice but to follow him.

The innkeeper was just serving one of the other guests, but when he was ready, John showed his money indicating that he wanted to pay him. The man shook his head and took them back to their table. There he motioned them to sit down and disappeared to his other guests.

"It seems to me that he wants us to wait," Manette gave as her opinion. "Maybe he has sent a message to someone who speaks French."

After a long time of sitting and watching the customers come and go, the door of the room opened again and a different kind of visitor entered. It was a stately man, dressed in black with a friendly round face. With a loud voice that boomed through the room he asked the innkeeper something. The innkeeper answered and pointed to the children. The man walked right to their table and grabbed an empty chair and seated himself with them.

The children watched him expectantly and were delighted when he began to talk in their own language. True, he had some kind of foreign accent but was easy to understand. He said that the innkeeper had sent a message to him that some Huguenot children had come. He explained that he was a minister of the Reformed Church in Vlissingen and had come as soon as possible to find out if they needed any help. It had taken him longer than he had expected for he first had to visit a few sick members of the congregation. However, now he had come and was ready to listen.

First he asked their names. When he discovered that the children were so intimidated by his booming voice that they didn't dare to say much, he began asking questions. Very soon they lost their shyness and began telling him all their adventures.

It took a long time before they were through with their story, but the minister listened patiently, and sometimes interrupted them with a question. After he'd heard most of the story, he said that he was glad to hear that there were still people in France who didn't deny the Lord Jesus Christ and had the courage to flee, trusting that the Lord would help them. He added that they had done well by persevering and patted John and Camille approvingly on their shoulders because they had helped Manette escape.

When the minister stopped talking, John, who felt that it was now his turn to get some more information, asked politely if the minister knew any other Huguenots, and if so, if he could help contact them for they needed their advice about what they should do next. The minister nodded approvingly and explained that no Huguenots were living in Vlissingen. Most of them were living in Amsterdam, where they even had worship services in a large church.[22] He understood fully that the children were very anxious to go there but advised them to stay in the inn for the next few days. They didn't have to worry about their meals or a place to sleep for now they were in Holland and he, the minister, would look after them as long as needed.

"The first thing to do is to get some decent clothes for all of you because you look like a set of beggars. Manette especially needs a nice dress, for it isn't good for a girl to walk around in boy's clothing. The sooner she gets rid of them the better."

"True," the boys admitted. "We'll buy a dress for her right away. Where can we find a store where they understand French?"

"Oh no, you don't have to do that," the minister replied, amused that the boys were in such a hurry. "You have to learn to economize. I doubt that you have a lot of money to spend. You know what? Tonight I'll sent somebody with some good clothing. They won't be new, of course, but good enough to use for the time being. In the meantime you can all stay here during the next few days for I have to notify the City Council that you are here. They will take this matter up and decide what to do with you."

Without waiting for a reply, he turned around on his chair and called with his booming voice, "Hannes!"

The innkeeper, who was busy at the other side of the room, looked up directly and came toward them.

After a short conversation with the innkeeper, the minister told the children that everything had been arranged. Manette could sleep

---

[22] Many Huguenots had fled to Germany, England, and The Netherlands. They received many privileges in The Netherlands. For example, they were exempt from taxes for many years, and the city of Amsterdam paid for the building of their houses.

in the same room as the maidservant, and the boys could sleep in an unoccupied guest room. They could also have the regular meals in the inn and didn't have to pay anything. Others would take care of that. He expected them to give a hand where possible! As a matter of fact, it would help them to learn Dutch. He invited them the next day to have lunch at his house because he wanted to introduce them to his wife.

The children thanked him abundantly for his help, but he didn't want to hear of it for he was, as he said, a servant of the same Lord Whom they followed, and with these words he left the inn.

Two days later, the secretary of the City Council wrote in the minutes of the council meeting that they had approved the setting aside of sufficient funds for sending the children to Amsterdam. The council members were "moved very deeply after having heard all the perils, the children had endured for the sake of our Lord Jesus Christ and the wonderful guidance given by Him so that the children would be instructed and kept in the teachings of His Church."

21

JOURNEY'S END

It was night in Amsterdam, the great merchant city of The Netherlands. All the busy activity of the day had come to a standstill and everybody had gone to bed. The days started so early that one really needed all the sleep he could get! But not everybody was asleep, for on the third floor of one of the houses a boy was quietly looking out of a window. It was John. He was supposed to be in bed a long time ago, but wasn't in the mood for it. So many exciting decisions had been made that day that he wanted to think them over again, especially because he was thankful that everything had ended so very well.

They had arrived in Amsterdam approximately three weeks ago, traveling like rich people, first by boat and next by mail coach, thanks to the money supplied by the City Council of Vlissingen. They were received by one of their countrymen, who had told them that he was the minister of the French Reformed Church. He had taken them home, where they met his friendly wife and for hours they had to tell about their adventures in France.

The following day had been Sunday and they had gone to church with the minister and his wife. It was a strange but happy experience to sit in a church with a great number of Huguenots, hearing the explanation of a Bible text by an able man. It was wonderful that nobody needed to be afraid of being put in jail or being persecuted.

After the worship service they were asked to recount the story of their escape to the whole congregation, and everybody listened with joy how the Lord had safely guided them. The event that impressed the children most during the service was that the minister remembered them in his prayer, thanking the Lord for His help. At that moment even John had felt tears in his eyes, not because he was sad but because he was so very glad!

The next day, the minister and his wife had sat down with them to discuss what they should do in the future. Clearly, the childless couple had fallen in love with Manette and the minister appeared to

174

be somewhat hesitant in his advice, afraid they would lose her. The wife of the minister suggested after some talking that they would stay with them during the next few weeks and take a very good rest. Afterward, it would perhaps be easier to decide what to do.

Today, at last, decisions had been made. The minister and his wife didn't like to separate brother and sister, but didn't know how they could keep them both on his rather small salary. When he hesitantly suggested that they had to be separated, all three protested vehemently. However, they calmed down very soon and even began to smile when the minister and his wife suggested that they would keep Manette and added that they would be happy if they would all agree with it because they loved her already as their own daughter.

"Our real problem is what to do with you, boys," the minister said. During the following discussion, Camille suddenly mentioned that he wanted very much to be a minister. Then he could later return to France and bring the gospel to his parents and all other people who might be willing to listen.

It was surely a great surprise for John. They had been such good friends all along that he thought he knew Camille thoroughly but he had never had an inkling of this desire. When he said so, Camille blushed and said that he had thought about it ever since they had been in Paris. He had never had the courage to mention it, though, afraid that John would make fun of it because he knew so very little of the Bible. But now things had changed. They were in a country with schools and universities and he would like to grasp this opportunity to study. He had always loved books and would be willing to give up everything if he only could become a minister. He asked the minister if it was possible to study and at the same time to work for a living.

The minister, who had listened with a happy smile on his face, assured him that they would undoubtedly find a way if he was serious about the ministry.

John wasn't sure what he wanted to do. His first thought was for his father whom he would like to find, but the minister said that such a thing was quite impossible. He told John that some of their friends would do their utmost to contact him, and maybe John could help later. He explained that it happened sometimes that galley slaves got permission to go ashore and to send letters, if they had enough money to pay for it. Several well-to-do Dutchmen, sincere Christians, did everything in their power to bring relief to the Huguenots on the galleys. They would try to get information from his father and help him.

Hearing this, John had asked the minister for advice about how he could best make a living for Manette and himself. He didn't like the idea of the minister and his wife paying everything for Manette because they could hardly afford it. The minister's wife had smiled and had said that she appreciated his regard for Manette and that she had a suggestion. Considering everything, she felt it would be better if John also stayed with them. As soon as he had a job, half of his wages could be used for food and clothing for Manette and himself, and the other half would pay for his studies. It was a good idea to have a job, she declared, but he shouldn't neglect his study for she was sure that it would be good for him to brush up his reading, writing, and arithmetic.

And then she had come with a real great surprise. If he wanted to go into business, she would contact an Amsterdam merchant who needed an office boy. She knew him well and was sure that he would take John if she asked him, especially because John spoke French.

As he sat in the window sill, he couldn't help feeling delighted about the wonderful way everything had been settled. Leaving Camille couldn't be helped, but he lived close by with another family from the church. Everything had worked out so well that he wondered sometimes if he was dreaming. God had made them forget all their fears and worries by providing for them abundantly! Impulsively he knelt down at the open window and gave thanks to Him Who had guided them through all the dangers of their escape to this country of freedom where they could confess His Name without being persecuted.

176

APPENDIX

HISTORY OF THE CHURCH REFORMATION IN FRANCE

The history of the Church of Christ in France is relatively unknown in spite of its glorious past. The faithful perseverance and testimony of its members through horrible persecutions are a source of praise and encouragement for all Christians. The courage and steadfastness of the French children, in particular during these gruesome years, have been unequalled during all the known history of the Church of Christ. Even now they are bright examples for all Christian teenagers, who in an anti-christian world are under serious peer pressure and exposed to the temptations of alcohol, drugs, and a deteriorated morality.

The following is a brief description of the early history of the Church of Christ in France.

The Protestants in France were named Huguenots. The true meaning of this name is not certain, but the word is probably derived from a word that means Covenanters.

The gospel spread fast after the beginning of the Reformation in Germany in 1517. In cooperation with the French kings, the mighty Roman Catholic Church tried its utmost to stop the progress of the Reformation using blatant persecutions. The first French martyr, an Augustinian monk, named Jean Valliers, was burned alive at the stake in Paris in 1523. It was the start of severe persecution in which thousands and thousands of Christians, men and women, children and old men, laymen and clergy were tortured and burned alive. Many historical sources tell of their faithful adherence to the Lord Jesus Christ.

The suffering in France was borne with Psalm singing. The death of the martyrs was a singing death; they sang while being burned alive. The Psalms of these Christian witnesses, sung in smoke and fire, became known. Everybody began to sing them.

Even in Paris one day three or four thousand people sang them in public despite the rage of the king.

The persecutions did not stop the progress of the Gospel. Less than thirty years after the death of the first martyr the Huguenot Church had nearly half a million members and a few years later at least forty percent of the total French population were Huguenots.

The first synod met in Paris in 1559. Obviously, they had to meet in secret because during those times, the Kings Francis I (1515-1547) and Henry II (1547-1550) tried to liquidate the Church. In spite of these difficulties, the synod was able to complete a heavy and important workload. It agreed upon a creed and established rules for governing the church, all based on Calvinistic, Biblical principles.

During this period a large number of nobles joined the Huguenot Church. Their leader was the well-known Caspard de Coligny. They were opposed by the Romanist nobles and their leader, De Guise. King Charles IX (1560-1574), who was wholly under the influence of his mother, Catherine de Medici, sided with the Romanists.

The struggle between these two parties came to an end with the bloody St. Bartholomew's night (Aug. 23-24, 1572). During that night and the next few days more than thirty thousand Huguenots were murdered, including De Coligny.

Until 1589 France was ravaged by civil war, murder and persecution. During that year, the protestant leader King Henry IV made a compromise; he became a Roman Catholic convert, and was acknowledged as France's legal king by both parties.

His main goal was then to maintain peace in his country, and so he gave special privileges to the Huguenots in the Edict of Nantes (1598). It allowed a kind of freedom of religion unknown in the western world, except in The Netherlands. The Huguenots were allowed to practice their religion in a certain number of cities, and they were recognized — to a certain extent — as an armed political party. In addition, they received some fortified towns, like the harbor town of La Rochelle.

However, these special privileges quickly became a threat to the very existence of the nation because the Huguenots were allowed to form their own state inside the nation. Cardinal Richelieu (1585-1642), then Prime Minister, understood this well. Gradually he canceled all privileges and conquered the fortified cities of the Huguenots.

Severe persecution of the Huguenots resumed during the reign of Louis XIV, the Sun King (1643-1715), because he wanted to be an absolute monarch. He expected to achieve his goal by allowing only one church in France, the Roman Catholic Church. He followed the recommendations of his confessor, the notorious Pere La Chaise, and supported any action that would result in the Huguenots returning to the Roman Church, including persecution, bribery, and murder.

The life of the Huguenots became unbearable after the revocation of the Edict of Nantes, and many of them tried to leave France. King Louis, who knew that the Huguenots were his most diligent and hard working subjects, did not want them to leave and used his soldiers to turn them back at the borders. Our story took place during those times.

In spite of the soldiers, approximately one-half million Huguenots succeeded in their flight. They were received and supported by the Christians in Switzerland, England, The Netherlands, and Brandenburg.

In the famous war of the Camisards (1702-1704), the Huguenots in a mountainous country of southern France called the Cevennes, tried to defend their lives. They are known as Camisards because they often wore a shirt (camisole) over their clothes during nightly attacks. Their courage and discipline were unrivalled. Although their army consisted of fewer than two thousand five hundred soldiers, a French army of twenty thousand men with famous generals and supported by fifty-two battalions of recruits could barely subdue them.

After this war, the Reformed Church in France appeared to be completely liquidated. However, after a few years a revival occurred and although the persecution continued, it was less bloody than before. At last, in 1790, the Huguenots were given freedom of religion. Even now the French Reformed Church is still active in its mission work, but continues to be very small.

Other Books from Inheritance Publications

Quintus by R. Weerstand
A Story About the Persecution of Christians
at the Time of Emperor Nero

The history of the Church in A.D. 64 is written with blood and tears. This book, based on historical facts, relates what happened in Rome in the summer of that year. It is a gripping chronicle. In the story we meet Quintus, the central character. He is a typical Roman boy, who through a number of ordeals experiences the grace of God.

Time: A.D. 64   Age: 12-99
Cat. Nr. IP 1270   Can.$8.95 U.S.$7.90

William of Orange - The Silent Prince
by W.G. Van de Hulst

F. Pronk in *The Messenger*: If you have ever wondered why Dutch Reformed people of former generations felt such strong spiritual ties with Dutch royalty, this is a "must" reading. In simple story form, understandable for children ages 10 and up, the Dutch author, wellknown for Christian children's literature, relates the true story of the origin of Dutch royalty. It all began with William of Nassau (1533-1584) . . . He dedicated his life and lost it for the cause of maintaining and promoting Protestantism in The Netherlands.

for age 9 - 99   ISBN 0-921100-15-9 Can.$8.95 U.S.$7.90

Salt in His Blood
The Life of Michael De Ruyter
by William R. Rang

The greatest Dutch Admiral is an example of Christian love and piety, and fascinating because of his many true adventures as a sailer-boy, captain, and pirate-hunter.

Time: 1607 - 1676   Age: 10-99
ISBN 0-921100-59-0   Can.$10.95 U.S.$9.90

Anak, the Eskimo Boy by Piet Prins

F. Pronk in *The Messenger*: Anak is an Eskimo Boy, who with his family, lives with the rest of their tribe in the far north. The author describes their day-to-day life as they hunt for seals, caribou and walruses. Anak is being prepared to take up his place as an adult and we learn how he is introduced to the tough way of life needed to survive in the harsh northern climate. We also learn how Anak and his father get into contact with the white man's civilization. . . This book makes fascinating reading, teaching about the ways of Eskimos, but also of the power of the Gospel. Anyone over eight years old will enjoy this book and learn from it.

for age 8 - 99   ISBN 0-921100-11-6 Can.$6.95 U.S.$6.30

Golden Inheritance Series #1
Jessica's First Prayer & Jessica's Mother
by Hesba Stretton

Liz Buist in *Reformed Perspective*: There is much to be learned from this story. It is written primarily for children, but this book is worthwhile reading for adults as well . . . Highly recommended for young and older.

The Sword and Trowel says (about *Jessica's First Prayer*): One of the most tender, touching, and withal gracious stories that we ever remember to have read. A dear little book for our children. We are not ashamed of having shed tears while reading it; in fact, should have been ten times more ashamed if we had not. The sweet portrait of the poor child Jessica is a study, and old Daniel is perfect in his own way.

Subject: Fiction   **Age: 9-99**
ISBN 0-921100-63-9   **Can.$8.95 U.S.$7.90**

Golden Inheritance Series #2 *Probable Sons* by Amy Le Feuvre

The *Sword and Trowel* says: A lovely story that everybody — man, woman, boy, or girl — ought to read. The heroine is a charming child who, in a most winning way, applies to everyday life the Parable of the Prodigal Son, whom she mis-calls the Probable Son. It is scarcely possible to praise too highly this delightful volume.

Subject: Fiction   **Age: 8-99**
ISBN 0-921100-81-7   **Can.$6.95 U.S.$5.90**

Golden Inheritance Series #3 *Pilgrim Street* by Hesba Stretton

Little Phil desperately wants to see his brother Tom. He knows Tom isn't guilty. But Phil is afraid of the policeman. Who will help these street urchins?

Subject: Fiction   **Age: 9-99**
ISBN 0-921100-91-4   **Can.$8.95 U.S.$7.90**

Golden Inheritance Series #4
Legend Led by Amy Le Feuvre

Christine Farenhorst in *Christian Renewal*: Three children, orphaned at an early age and living with a governess, are suddenly sent for by an older step-brother who lives in the country. Steeped in Arthurian legends, Gypsy, the youngest of the three children, is convinced that the Holy Grail, or 'Holy Thing' as she calls it, is hidden somewhere on their brother's estate. When she does actually find the 'Holy Thing', it is not quite what she has expected. Reminiscent of W.G. VandeHulst, this book is sure to endear itself to parents as well as to young children. Most certainly recommended.

Subject: Fiction   **Age: 10-99**
ISBN 0-921100-82-5   **Can.$8.95 U.S.$7.90**

When The Morning Came by Piet Prins
Struggle for Freedom Series 1

D. Engelsma in the *Standard Bearer*: This is reading for Reformed children, young people, and (if I am any indication) their parents. It is the story of 12-year-old Martin Meulenberg and his family during the Roman Catholic persecution of the Reformed Christians in The Netherlands about the year 1600. A peddlar, secretly distributing Reformed books from village to village, drops a copy of Guido de Brès' *True Christian Confession* — a booklet forbidden by the Roman Catholic authorities. An evil neighbor sees the book and informs . . .

for age 9 - 99   **ISBN 0-921100-12-4   Can.$9.95 U.S.$8.90**

Dispelling the Tyranny by Piet Prins
Struggle for Freedom Series 2

"Father! Mother! I saw Count Lodewyk! He rode through the city on a black horse!" Martin shouted, as he dashed into the humble home where his parents were eating supper. "The cavalry followed him, and everywhere he went the people cheered him on!" Martin's eyes sparkled with excitement.

for age 9 - 99

ISBN 0-921100-40-X   Can.$9.95   U.S.$8.90

Augustine, The Farmer's Boy of Tagaste by P. De Zeeuw

C. MacDonald in *The Banner of Truth*: Augustine was one of the

great teachers of the Christian Church, defending it against many heretics. This interesting publication should stimulate and motivate all readers to extend their knowledge of Augustine and his works.

J. Sawyer in *Trowel & Sword*: . . . It is informative, accurate historically and theologically, and very readable. My daughter loved it (and I enjoyed it myself). An excellent choice for home and church libraries.

Time: 354 - 430 A.D.   **Age: 9-99**

ISBN 0-921100-05-1   **Can.$7.95 U.S.$6.90**

The Escape by A. Van der Jagt
The Adventures of Three Huguenot Children
Fleeing Persecution

F. Pronk in *The Messenger*: This book . . . will hold its readers spellbound from beginning to end. The setting is late seventeenth century France. Early in the story the mother dies and the father is banished to be a galley slave for life on a war ship. Yet in spite of threats and punishment, sixteen-year-old John and his ten-year-old sister Manette, refuse to give up the faith they have been taught.

Time: 1685 - 1695   **Age: 12-99**
ISBN 0-921100-04-3   **Can.$11.95 U.S.$9.95**

The Secret Mission by A. Van der Jagt
A Huguenot's Dangerous Adventures
in the Land of Persecution

In the sequel to our best-seller, *The Escape,* John returns to France with a secret mission of the Dutch Government. At the same time he attempts to find his father.

Time: 1702-1712   **Age: 12-99**
ISBN 0-921100-18-3   **Can.$14.95 U.S.$10.95**

How They Kept The Faith
by Grace Raymond
A Tale of the Huguenots of Languedoc

Eglantine and Rene grew up together in a Huguenot family. Already at a young age they are committed to become each other's life's partner. When persecution breaks out they each must endure their individual struggles to remain faithful to God and to each other. A must for teenagers and adults.

Time: 1676 - 1686   **Age: 13-99**
ISBN 0-921100-64-7   **Can.$14.95 U.S.$12.90**

The Young Huguenots by Edith S. Floyer
It was a happy life at the pretty chateau. Even after that dreadful Sunday evening, when strange men came down and shut the people out of the church, not much changed for the four children. Until the soldiers came . . .

Time: 1686 - 1687   **Age: 11-99**
ISBN 0-921100-65-5   **Can.$11.95 U.S.$9.90**

The Shadow Series
by Piet Prins

One of the most exciting series of a master story teller about the German occupation of The Netherlands during the emotional time of the Second World War (1940-1945).

K. Bruning in *Una Sancta* about Vol.4 - The Partisans, and Vol. 5 - Sabotage: . . . the country was occupied by the German military forces. The nation's freedom was destroyed by the foreign men in power. Violence, persecutions and executions were the order of the day, and the main target of the enemy was the destruction of the christian way of life. In that time the resistance movement of underground fighters became very active. People from all ages and levels joined in and tried to defend the Dutch Christian heritage as much as possible. The above mentioned books show us how older and younger people were involved in that dangerous struggle. It often was a life and death battle. Every page of these books is full of tension. The stories give an accurate and very vivid impression of that difficult and painful time. These books should also be in the hands of our young people. They are excellent instruments to understand the history of their own country and to learn the practical value of their own confession and Reformed way of life. What about as presents on birthdays?

Time: 1944-1945   **Age: 10-99**

Vol. 1 The Lonely Sentinel
ISBN 0-88815-781-9
Can.$7.95 U.S.$6.35

Vol. 2 Hideout in the Swamp
ISBN 0-88815-782-7
Can.$7.95 U.S.$6.35

Vol. 3 The Grim Reaper
ISBN 0-88815-783-5
Can.$6.95 U.S.$5.65

Vol. 4 The Partisans
ISBN 0-921100-07-8
Can.$7.95 U.S.$7.20

Vol. 5 Sabotage
ISBN 0-921100-08-6
Can.$7.95 U.S.$7.20

Coronation of Glory by **Deborah Meroff**
"Miss Meroff . . . has fictionalized the story of Lady Jane Grey in a thoroughly absorbing manner . . . she has succeeded in making me believe this is what really happened. I kept wanting to read on — the book is full of action and interest."
— *Elisabeth Elliot*
The true story of seventeen-year-old Lady Jane Grey, Queen of England for nine days.

Time: 1537-1554   **Age: 14-99**
ISBN 0-921100-78-7   **Can.\$14.95 U.S.\$12.90**

The Romance of Protestantism by **Deborah Alcock**
The Romance of Protestantism addresses one of the most damaging and (historically) effective slanders against the Reformed faith, which is that it is cold and doctrinaire. What a delight to find a book which documents the true warmth of the Protestant soul. I recommend this book highly.
— Douglas Wilson, editor of *Credenda/Agenda*
Time: 1390-1800   **Age: 12-99**
ISBN 0-921100-88-4   **Can.\$9.95 U.S.\$8.90**

The Spanish Brothers by **Deborah Alcock**
A Tale of the Sixteenth Century
Christine Farenhorst in *Christian Renewal*:
This historical novel which is set in Spain a number of years after the Reformation, deals with the discovery of Reformed truth in that country. It's not often that we come across a book that touches upon people and places with regard to Biblical truth in Spain. As a matter of fact, we generally think of Spain as one of the most zealous and fiery arms of the Inquisition. Yet Spain itself most certainly also had its own martyrs and heroes of the faith. For this reason alone, the book would be a worthwhile read - to acquaint people with the historical facts of the rise and fall of the early Protestant church in Spain.

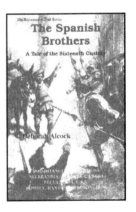

Two brothers, one a soldier and the other a student of theology, are the protagonists. Sons of a nobleman who disappeared when they were children, their search for him leads both to a confrontation with the Gospel. How they react, how their friends and relatives react to them, and what their struggles and thoughts are, form the main body of the book.
An excellent read, this book should be in every church and home library.
Time: 1550-1565   **Age: 14-99**
ISBN 1-984666-02-x   **Can.\$14.95 U.S.\$12.90**

The Word of the King Series

Abraham's

Cor Van Rijswijk
Illustrated by Rino Visser

Abraham's Sacrifice by Cor Van Rijswijk

Abraham was rich.
He had many cows and sheep, donkeys and camels.
He also had lots of gold and silver.
The Lord had given him all these animals and things.

This book is part of The Word of the King Series.
The purpose of this series is to present Bible stories in such a fashion that young children can read them.
Read them to your four or five-year-old, and let your six or seven-year-old use them as readers.

Time: Abraham **Age: 4-8**
ISBN 1-984666-21-6 Can.$8.95 U.S.$7.90

Little Meg's Children by Hesba Stretton

"Oh, if you please, Mr. Police," said Meg, in a plaintive voice, "I want to get these two little children over to the other side, and I don't know how to do it, except if you would please hold baby while I take Robbie across." The policeman looked down from his great height, without bending his stiff neck, upon the childish creature who spoke to him, and Meg's spirit sank with the fear of being ordered back again. But he picked up Robin under his arm, and bidding her keep close beside him, he threaded his way through the throng of carriages. This was the last danger; and now with restored gaiety Meg travelled on with her two children.

Golden Inheritance Series # 5

Little Meg's Children

Hesba Stretton

INHERITANCE PUBLICATIONS
NEERLANDIA, ALBERTA, CANADA
PELLA, IOWA, U.S.A.
ROMSEY, HANTS, UNITED KINGDOM

Subject: Fiction **Age: 9-99**
ISBN 0-921100-92-2 Can.$8.95 U.S.$7.90

Hubert Ellerdale
A Tale of the Days of Wycliffe

W. Oak Rhind

ROMSEY, HANTS, UNITED KINGDOM

Hubert Ellerdale by W. Oak Rhind
A Tale of the Days of Wycliffe

Christine Farenhorst in *Christian Renewal*: Christians often tend to look on the Reformation as the pivotal turning point in history during which the Protestants took off the chains of Rome. This small work of fiction draws back the curtains of history a bit further than Luther's theses. Wycliffe was the morning star of the Reformation and his band of Lollards a band of faithful men who were persecuted because they spoke out against salvation by grace alone. Hubert Ellerdale was such a man and his life, (youth, marriage and death), albeit fiction, is set parallel to Wycliffe's and Purvey's.
Rhind writes with pathos and the reader can readily identify with his lead characters. This novel deserves a well-dusted place in a home, school or church library.

Time: 1380-1420 **Age: 13-99**
ISBN 0-921100-09-4 Can.$12.95 U.S.$10.90

Against the World - The Odyssey of Athanasius by Henry W. Coray

Muriel R. Lippencott in *The Christian Observer*: [it] . . . is a partially fictionalized profile of the life of Athanasius . . . who died in A.D. 373. Much of the historical content is from the writing of reliable historians. Some parts of the book, while the product of the author's imagination, set forth accurately the spirit and the temper of the times, including the proceedings and vigorous debates that took place in Alexandria and Nicea. . . This is the story that Rev. Coray so brilliantly tells.

Time: A.D. 331-373　　　　　　　　　　　　　**Age: 16-99**
ISBN 0-921100-35-3　　　　　　　　**Can.$8.95 U.S.$7.90**

With Wolfe in Canada by G.A. Henty

Through misadventure the hero of the story James Walsham, becomes involved in the historic struggle between Britain and France for supremacy on the North American continent. The issue of this war determined not only the destinies of North America, but to a large extent those of the mother countries themselves. With Wolfe in Canada will take the reader through many battles of this conflict. Meet a young George Washington and General Braddock as they fight the French and Indians, join up with Rogers' Rangers, and learn of the legendary generals Wolfe and Montcalm. With Wolfe in Canada is a model of what a children's book should be with its moving tale of military exploit and thrilling adventure. This classic provides a lesson in history instructively and graphically, whilst infusing into the dead facts of history new life. Mr. Henty's classic With Wolfe in Canada is a useful aid to study as well as amusement.

Time: 1750-1765　　　　　　　　　　　　　**Age: 14-99**
Cloth ISBN 0-921100-86-8　　　　　**Can.$28.95 U.S.$19.99**
Paperback ISBN 0-921100-87-6　　　**Can.$20.95 U.S.$13.99**

Journey Through the Night by Anne De Vries

After the second world war, Anne De Vries, one of the most popular novelists in The Netherlands, was commissioned to capture in literary form the spirit and agony of those five harrowing years of Nazi occupation. The result was Journey Through the Night, a four volume bestseller that has gone through more than thirty printings in The Netherlands.

"An Old Testament Professor of mine who bought the books could not put them down — nor could I."

— Dr. Edwin H. Palmer

Time: 1940-1945　　　　　　　　　　　　　**Age: 10-99**
ISBN 1-984666-21-6　　　　　　　　**Can.$19.95 U.S.$14.90**

The Soldier of Virginia - A Novel on George Washington by Marjorie Bowen

"Mr. Washington — and who is Mr. Washington?"

"It is the Governor of Virginia's envoy, Monsieur — bearing a letter from his Excellency."

St. Pierre gave his inferior officer a quick glance; two things occurred to him: the first was that Dinwiddie must be serious if he had sent a messenger in such weather; the second was that it would have been more courteous if the envoy had been a man of some rank; he remarked on neither of these things, but quietly requested that Mr. Washington should be brought into his presence.

The scene was St. Pierre's room in the newly erected Fort le Bœuf; December cold filled the apartment despite the huge fire of logs that roared on the hearth; and the view from the window was of a frozen lake, great trees against a drab sky, and the steady falling of snowflakes.

Originally published in 1912, this is a fictionalized biography on America's first President by one of the best authors of historical fiction.

Time: 1755-1775   Age: 14-99
ISBN 0-921100-99-X   Can.$ 14.95 U.S.$ 12.90

The Governor of England by Marjorie Bowen
A Novel on Oliver Cromwell

An historical novel in which the whole story of Cromwell's dealings with Parliament and the King is played out. It is written with dignity and conviction, and with the author's characteristic power of grasping the essential details needed to supply colour and atmosphere for the reader of the standard histories.

Time: 1645-1660   Age: 14-99
ISBN 0-921100-58-2   Can.$17.95 U.S.$15.90

Israel's Hope and Expectation by Rudolf Van Reest

G. Nederveen in *Clarion*: This is one of the best novels I have read of late. I found it captivating and hard to put down. Here is a book that is not time-bound and therefore it will never be outdated.

The story takes place around the time of Jesus' birth. It is written by someone who has done his research about the times between the Old and New Testament period. The author informs you in an easy style about the period of the Maccabees. . . Van Reest is a good storyteller. His love for the Bible and biblical times is evident from the start. He shows a good knowledge of the customs and mannerisms in Israel. Many fine details add to the quality of the book. You will be enriched in your understanding of the ways in the Old Testament.

Time: Inter-Testament Period   Age: 15-99
ISBN 0-921100-22-1   Can.$19.95 U.S.$17.90

The William & Mary Trilogy
by Marjorie Bowen

The life of William III, Prince of Orange, Stadtholder of the United Netherlands, and King of England (with Queen Mary II) is one of the most fascinating in all of history. Both the author and the publisher of this book have been interested in this subject for many years. Although the story as told in this book is partly fictional, all the main events are faithful to history. F. Pronk wrote in *The Messenger* about Volume 1:

The author is well-known for her well-researched fiction based on the lives of famous historical characters. The religious convictions of the main characters are portrayed with authenticity and integrity. This book is sure to enrich one's understanding of Protestant Holland and will hold the reader spell-bound.

D.J. Engelsma wrote in *The Standard Bearer* about Volume 1: This is great reading for all ages, high school and older. *I Will Maintain* is well written historical fiction with a solid, significant, moving historical base . . . No small part of the appeal and worth of the book is the lively account of the important history of one of the world's greatest nations, the Dutch.

This history was bound up with the Reformed faith and had implications for the exercise of Protestantism throughout Europe. Christian high schools could profitably assign the book, indeed, the whole trilogy, for history or literature classes.

C. Farenhorst wrote in *Christian Renewal* about Volume 1: An excellent tool for assimilating historical knowledge without being pained in the process, *I Will Maintain* is a very good read. Take it along on your holidays. Its sequel *Defender of the Faith*, is much looked forward to.

Time: 1670 - 1702   Age: 14-99

Volume 1 - *I Will Maintain*
          ISBN 0-921100-42-6   Can.$17.95 U.S.$15.90
Volume 2 - *Defender of the Faith*
          ISBN 0-921100-43-4   Can.$15.95 U.S.$13.90
Volume 3 - *For God and the King*
          ISBN 0-921100-44-2   Can.$17.95 U.S.$15.90

Servant of Slaves by Grace Irwin
A Biographical Novel of John Newton

This is Grace Irwin's best novel to date. She recounts the exciting adventures of John Newton's life both as profane and immoral slave trader and later as a devoted servant of Christ. And is there anywhere a more beautiful love story than that of John Newton and Mary Catlett? — Clyde S. Kilby

Time: 1725-1807   **Age: 14-99**
ISBN 0-88815-908-0   **Can.$11.95 U.S.$9.95**

The Seventh Earl
by Grace Irwin

A dramatized biography on Anthony Ashley Cooper, the Seventh Earl of Shaftesbury, who is most widely remembered as a 19th-century British philanthropist and factory reformer. "This is Grace Irwin's strongest and most poignant book . . . I have been moved and enriched by my hours with *The Seventh Earl*," wrote V.R. Mollenkott.

Time: 1801-1885   **Age: 14-99**
ISBN 0-8028-6059-1   **Can.$11.95 U.S.$9.95**

A Stranger in a Strange Land
by Leonora Scholte

John E. Marshall in *The Banner of Truth*: This is a delightful book. It tells the story of H.P. Scholte, a preacher in The Netherlands, who being persecuted for his faith in his own country, emigrated to the U.S.A., and there established a settlement in Pella, Iowa, in the midst of the vast undeveloped prairie. . . The greater part of the book is taken up in telling the stories of the immense hardships known after emigration. Interwoven with this story is an account of Scholte's marriage and family life. . . It is a most heartwarming and instructive story.

Time: 1825-1880   **Age: 14-99**
ISBN 0-921100-01-9   **Can.$7.95 U.S.$6.90**

Captain My Captain by Deborah Meroff
author of *Coronation of Glory*

Willy-Jane VanDyken in *The Trumpet*: This romantic novel is so filled with excitement and drama, it is difficult to put it down once one has begun it. Its pages reflect the struggle between choosing Satan's ways or God's ways. Mary's struggles with materialism, being a submissive wife, coping with the criticism of others, learning how to deal with sickness and death of loved ones, trusting in God and overcoming the fear of death forces the reader to reflect on his own struggles in life.

This story of Mary Ann Patten (remembered for being the first woman to take full command of a merchant sailing ship) is one that any teen or adult reader will enjoy. It will perhaps cause you to shed a few tears but it is bound to touch your heart and encourage you in your faith.

Time: 1837-1861   **Age: 14-99**
ISBN 0-921100-79-5   **Can.$14.95 U.S.$12.90**

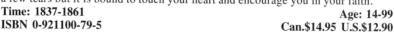

Love in Times of Reformation by **William P. Balkenende**

N.N. in *The Trumpet*: This historical novel plays in The Netherlands during the rise of the protestant Churches, under the persecution of Spain, in the latter half of the sixteenth century. Breaking with the Roman Catholic Church in favor of the new faith is for many an intense struggle. Anthony Tharret, the baker's apprentice, faces his choice before the R.C. Church's influenced Baker's Guild. His love for Jeanne la Solitude, the French Huguenot refugee, gives a fresh dimension to the story. Recommended! Especially for young people.

Time: 1560-1585   **Age: 14-99**
ISBN 0-921100-32-9   **Can.$8.95 U.S.$7.90**

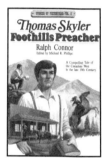

Thomas Skyler: Foothills Preacher
by **Ralph Connor**

A compelling tale of the Canadian West in the late 19th century by Ralph Connor. Meet Bronco Bill . . . Hi Kendal . . . the Duke . . . the Old Timer . . . and of course Gwen . . . and discover why the impact of "the Sky Pilot" was far different than any would have expected.

Subject: Fiction   **Age: 12-99**
ISBN 0-940652-07-2   **Can.$9.99 U.S.$7.90**

He Gathers the Lambs by
Cornelius Lambregtse

A moving book, written not only with deep insight into the ecclesiastical, religious, social, and historical situation in which the story takes place, but also with a warm, rich understanding of a child's soul. Every page of the book carries proof that it was eked out of the author's own experience. It is written from the inside out, and the people who appear in it are flesh-and-blood people as they walked the streets of southeastern Zeeland. Zeelanders with a mystical character . . . who had great difficulty appropriating in faith the redemptive deeds of the covenant God.

Also beautiful in this story are the descriptions of the natural beauty of the island on which it takes place. The author views nature with a loving but also with a knowledgeable eye. The landscape through all the seasons. . . But what is most striking is his knowledge of the soul of a child, a knowledge born out of love.   — Rudolf Van Reest

Subject: Fiction   **Age: 14-99**
ISBN 0-921100-77-9   **Can.$14.95 U.S.$12.90**

The Crown of Honour by **L. Erkelens**

Rachel Manesajian in *Chalcedon Report*: This book is about an illegitimate girl whose mother died when she was born, and no one knows who her father is. She grows up in an orphanage, and she goes through many hardships and is treated poorly because she is illegitimate. The few people she loves are taken away from her. Because of all her trials, she thinks God is against her, and so, in rebellion, she refuses to go to church or pray. However, the prayers of an old man who loves and prays for her are answered and she realizes . . . a wonderful story.

Subject: Fiction   **Age: 14-99**
ISBN 0-921100-14-0   **Can.$11.95 U.S.$10.90**

Judy's Own Pet Kitten by An Rook

Fay S. Lapka in *Christian Week*: Judy, presumably seven or eight years of age, is the youngest member of a farm family whose rural setting could be anywhere in Canada. The story of Judy, first losing her own kitten, then taming a wild stray cat with kittens, and finally rescuing the tiniest one from a flood, is well-told and compelling.

Subject: Fiction   **Age: 6-10**
ISBN 0-921100-34-5   **Can.$4.95 U.S.$4.50**

Susanneke by C. J. Van Doornik

Little Susanneke is happy! Tomorrow is Christmas. And Daddy has cleaned the church. But did he forget something? When it is her birthday Mommy always decorates the livingroom. And actually they will celebrate the Lord Jesus' birthday tomorrow. But the church isn't decorated at all. Could the big people have forgotten it? That is sad for the Lord. He loves us so much and now no one has thought about decorating the church for Him. She has to think about that for a moment. What should she do?

Subject: Fiction   **Age: 6-8**
ISBN 0-921100-61-2   **Can.$4.95 U.S.$4.50**

Tekko Series
by Alie Vogelaar

... You will watch a little African boy do his utmost to save his little sister. You will see his whole village turn against him. And you will see how God works in wondrous ways to help him. I highly recommend this book for parents to read to their young children, some parts are scary, or for older children to read themselves. — Rebecca Kingswood (*a grade five student*) in *Pioneer*.

Subject: Mission / Fiction   **Age: 8-99**

1 *Tekko and the White Man*   **ISBN 0-921100-47-7 Can.$7.95   U.S.$6.90**
2 *Tekko the Fugitive*   **ISBN 0-921100-74-4 Can.$7.95   U.S.$6.90**
3 *Tekko Returns*   **ISBN 0-921100-75-2 Can.$7.95   U.S.$6.90**